Fae Academies: The FGA

An Unlikely Match

A.J. CULEY

**She's a Fae Criminal
making True Love matches.
What could possibly go wrong?**

Mari expects to follow family tradition and continue her education as a career Criminal at the Fae High Crimes Academy. Instead, however, she's assigned to the Fae Godparent Academy where she's expected to learn everything there is to know about making True Love matches. This has to be a joke. Right?

Finn expects to become the top student in his class at the FGA, just like every other member of his family. Unfortunately, his lab partner for the year is Mari, who makes it clear she doesn't believe in True Love. Now the two of them are expected to work together to make the unlikeliest match of the century: the rebellious Cinderella with the arrogant Prince Charming.

It's going to be a very long year at the FGA.

Chapter One

AT AGE NINETY-six, a mere four years from adulthood, each and every Fae must take The Assessment, the results of which determine their life path. There is one day each year designated for The Assessment and most Fae in the weeks that follow anxiously await their results.

In my family, however, the results are always the same: Classification Criminal. And by always, I mean for as far back as our records go.

We Fae take our classifications very seriously. There's a hierarchy of power and Classification Criminal is almost at the very top.

It's perhaps a bit confusing to the other races, especially humans, who do not value their criminals, but in Fae society, we're viewed as both necessary and indispensable.

This doesn't necessarily mean we're accepted in polite company, of course. In fact, we're most often greeted with fear rather than any sort of welcome.

This doesn't make a whole lot of sense considering our victims are rarely the Fae themselves and the crimes we undertake are always with the good of the Fae in mind (and by the Fae, I mean the Throne of Faerie itself).

Of course, since we Criminals aren't much for polite company and indeed, rather enjoy being feared, we can't really complain at the results of our chosen profession (and by chosen, I mean conscripted based on our Assessment results).

I'm pretty sure other classifications are envious of our freedom. We don't have to worry about anything so pesky as morals and we get to wreak havoc the worlds over. Of all the Classifications, in fact, we Criminals have unlimited access to the worlds beyond the Veil.

It's probably something I should be grateful for. My mother's always telling me how lucky I am to have been born into such an influential family and that I'm practically guaranteed a life of greatness.

Right.

Greatness.

Assuming I don't get ground to dust as yet another Criminal cog caught in the wheel of the Fae.

I learned from a very early age that we Criminals might be deemed indispensable, but that doesn't mean we won't be sacrificed for the good of the Fae (and by Fae, yes, I do still mean the Throne of Faerie).

There are many different paths a Criminal might take, but ultimately, they all lead to the same destination.

Assassin? You'll be taking out the Throne's enemies until they manage to take you out instead.

Thief? You'll be stealing treasures for the Throne until you're caught and imprisoned for life. Or executed.

Toppler of regimes? Anarchist? Terrorist? Expect a violent death.

Most Fae live for centuries, well beyond ten in fact, but our Criminals either spend those centuries in prison or they die young. The truly unfortunate go insane.

I happen to be the youngest and the only girl in my family, and by only girl, I mean there are no records of a single female birth in the five millennia of my family's records.

By the time I was born, twelve of my brothers had spent centuries causing chaos, starting wars, overthrowing governments and stealing treasures from pretty much every civilization throughout the realms. They were also entirely dead. Most of them were barely into their second century when their violent lives were brought to an abrupt end.

In my third year of life, another brother was caught attempting to assassinate the king of some remote island and was executed.

In my seventh year of life, yet another brother was caught attempting to steal a magical artifact from a witches' coven and disappeared.

No one's seen or heard from him since.

Over the next ten years, one brother was imprisoned and another went insane and is currently confined to an asylum built to contain the Fae.

I have two brothers still living, though I'm not at all hopeful for their futures.

In case you got lost in the math, that's eighteen older brothers. Of course, I never met a single one, not even the two who are still alive. They're too busy causing chaos to come home, I guess

I really can't blame them. After all, the youngest of the eighteen is still three hundred years older than me. I was a bit of a surprise child, to say the least.

In fact, my father never knew my mother had gotten pregnant again. He was off manipulating some war in a faraway land when she found out. He then died in that same war mere days before my birth, a victim of his own machinations.

In her grief, my mother apparently went on a six-month bender, and when she returned to sanity, she discovered she was pregnant again. No one really knows who the father is, but the result was that I gained both a brother and a sister who are exactly eleven months younger than me.

In a random twist of fate, the twins and I, along with two of our cousins, all turned ninety-six before this year's Day of Assessment.

As a result, we all assessed together, and if things go according to plan, we'll be entering The Academy together as well. There are a number of academies among the Fae, but only one is known as *The* Academy and that's the one that trains Classification Criminal.

There isn't a lot of excitement in the house the morning the envelopes arrive, even though there are five of us who will be entering The Academy this year.

I'm surprised at the lack of excitement given my uncertainty about the twins. They're not of my father's blood, which means they could conceivably be conscripted into any of the Academies, even the FGA.

I'm actually quite worried we'll be split up.

They could each be pulled into separate academies and it's quite possible neither will be Classified Criminal.

No one else seems too worried, though, and when the mail arrives, no one even bothers to check it.

Finally, I go and fetch the mail myself and am tempted—quite tempted—to open the twins' envelopes to get a peek, so I can prepare them for disappointment if it comes.

I swallow hard and go into the house and offer the envelopes to my mother.

"Put them on the side table in the dining room. We'll open them after dinner," she tells me.

"What if the twins—"

"Don't borrow trouble, Mari. Now go."

I sigh and do as I'm told, though as I drop them on the table in the dining room, I'm tempted once more to take a peek.

I resist though.

Dinner is the usual raucous affair, with my cousins and half-brother attempting to outdo each other with their ridiculous stories of high crimes committed throughout the day (by high crimes, I mean idiotic mischief).

Eventually, toward the end of dinner, my cousin Dorian reaches back and grabs the envelopes from the side table. He passes them to my mother, who makes a big production of opening the first envelope.

"Blade." She smiles at my brother. "Blah-blah-blah. Pleased to inform you. Blah-blah-blah. Classification Criminal."

Everyone cheers and I let out a huge sigh of relief.

One down.

I hold my breath as she opens the second envelope.

"Malia." She smiles at my sister. "No surprise here. Classification Criminal."

Unbelievable. I feel like we've dodged a bayonet. I grin at Blade and Malia.

Fae High Crimes Academy, here we come.

"Dorian." My mother smiles at my cousin. "Classification Criminal."

I roll my eyes. Of course, we have to go through the same process for each envelope, even though the rest of the results are pretty much set in stone.

"Gabriel. Classification Criminal."

My mother sets aside Gabriel's letter and opens the final envelope. She smiles at me, then pulls out the paper to glance at it.

A long beat of silence follows.

"Marigold." She slowly raises her head to look down the table at me. "Classification Godparent."

Chapter Two

SILENCE HAS FALLEN in the dining room since my mother stormed out, promising to "eviscerate those idiots in Assessing."

My mother has a strict no mirrors, not even pocket ones, at the table, so she had to leave the room to fetch one.

She's been on the mirror, pacing through the main floor ever since.

Every once in a while, she storms past the dining room, shouting into her handheld as she tries to convince some bureaucrat somewhere to "fix this Faerie nonsense right this minute!"

"They must have made a mistake." Dorian breaks the silence that falls in my mother's wake. "No Dragonblades have *ever* been classified anything but Criminal."

I nod, but all I can think is that I'm the only known female Dragonblade to have ever been born. Malia may be female, but she's not a Dragonblade.

How ironic that the non-blooded sister made it into High Crimes

Academy while the blooded one has been relegated to the cushiest, lamest Academy of them all: the FGA, otherwise known as Fae Godparent Academy.

"It's ridiculous," Gabriel agrees. "There must have been a mix-up."

"They probably got your results and mine confused," Malia says.

I take one look at her and realize she's terrified. If it is a mistake and Malia is intended for the FGA, it will mean she's the one to be separated from me and our cousins and even worse, her twin.

"If there is a mistake, I doubt it has anything to do with you," I assure her. "After all, Blade made it into The Academy and he's your twin. It's rare for twins to be separated into different academies." Though not rare enough for my peace of mind.

"She's right," my Uncle Leon says. "No matter how the results ended up, you two were always destined for the same Academy."

I can't imagine anything worse than being separated from the twins and my cousins, unless it's having to learn how to use my magic to make matches among humans in the name of *True Love*.

Yeah, that's definitely worse.

Especially for someone like me. I don't believe in True Love and I definitely don't want it for myself *or* to have to spend my life manipulating others into believing they've found it.

What a nightmare!

I'm convinced my mother will be back any minute to say it was a mistake and everything's been fixed. My only concern is whether that fix will result in the twins being separated. If that's the case, I'll make the sacrifice and accept the placement.

"I'm positive a mistake has been made," my mother says as she sweeps back into the dining room. "Unfortunately, no one at the

Assessment Center is willing to admit it, which tells me there's more going on here than we know."

"What if it isn't a mistake?" Gabriel asks. "What if Mari really *is* supposed to be a Fae Godmother?"

I snicker. "Are you serious right now?"

Gabriel shrugs. "I mean, anything's possible, right?"

"Sure," I scoff. "And I suppose you believe the Fae deliver coins beneath pillows in exchange for teeth as well."

"Hey," Gabriel exclaims.

I shrug. "Just saying."

"Well, personally," Dorian says. "I can't think of a single person less likely to have been chosen for the True Love Academy."

I gag. "Don't call it that. *Please* don't call it that."

He hoots with laughter. "You can't even stand to hear the words. How on earth are you going to make matches that bring joy and wonder to the world?"

"Ugh." I drop my head to the table.

"I mean have you heard their propaganda?" Dorian demanded.

"Yeah, I don't even know why they bother since joining an Academy isn't really a choice," Malia said. "You're conscripted according to your test results and you graduate from the Academy and serve accordingly or you're exiled."

"Maybe exile wouldn't be so bad," I muse. "I could travel and see all the different worlds."

"You'd have to choose one world," Blade points out. "Without access to the Veil, you couldn't travel between them."

"And they wouldn't let you bring your mirrors," Malia says, "so we wouldn't be able to stay in touch."

Damn. They were right.

"Don't even think about it," my mother says. "You'll report to the FGA, you'll do all your assignments and perform at the top of your class and show them what a Dragonblade is made of."

"Uh, if she shows them what we're made of, you can pretty much expect all the matches to fail, some of the targets to catch fire and all the engagement and wedding rings to disappear," Dorian says.

My mother glares at him. "Fine. Valid point. Show them we Dragonblades can twist and turn and flex when needed. Show them you're to be feared even as you make the matches of the century. And while you're doing that, I'll be trying to get to the bottom of this debacle. Come, Mari. Walk with me." She stands and strides from the room.

I leap up and bolt after her.

"You're going to need to be on guard every minute," she says to me.

"Okay," I draw the word out slowly. "Are you saying you don't think this was a mistake?"

"That's exactly what I'm saying. But I also don't believe that your results indicated the FGA was an appropriate placement for you."

I can't even express the relief I feel when she says this. When she was off yelling on the mirror at bureaucrats, I had a moment of doubt, where I thought maybe a godparent was all I was supposed to be.

"So, this is either an attempt to hurt our family in some way, possibly by isolating you from the rest of the group in order to assassinate or kidnap you, or it's an attempt to get you to infiltrate the one Academy no Criminal has ever seen the inside of."

I freeze at the mere thought of it. "Do you think that's even possible? It would mean someone high up managed to corrupt someone inside the Assessment Center."

"Anything's possible when we're talking about the Fae, Mari."

She's right.

"I wish we had more time to strategize and make a plan, but the Fae Travel Guard arrives tomorrow at eight a.m. to escort each of you to your respective Academies."

"Typical," I say. "They never give any kind of notice at all."

"Which is why I've been telling you to pack for the past two weeks."

I grin. "And that's why I listened to you and am already packed."

She chuckles. "That's my Mari." She sweeps me into her arms and hugs me tight. "I will miss you, my Marigold. This house will seem empty without you and the twins in it."

Chapter Three

THE FOLLOWING MORNING, the platforms at the Shadowstorm Waystation, are filled to the brim with students waiting for their Academy's Travel Guard.

I'm sticking as close as I can to the twins and my cousins. I want to enjoy every minute of our time together before it all comes to an end. We already said our goodbyes to the rest of the family as only students are allowed on the platforms themselves.

This isn't exactly wonderful news because it means there are no families to provide a buffer between us and the other students.

This particular Waystation serves three territories so it's highly probable there are both Criminals and Godparents scattered throughout the crowds and I dread the moment they realize a famed Dragonblade will be attending the FGA.

It's hard to hide my status as a Dragonblade when the birthmark that comes with the blood is emblazoned on my left cheek. A dagger stretches from the edge of my eyebrow all the way down to my jawbone. A tiny dragon curls around the hilt and spews flames down across the blade.

I haven't yet managed to call the dragon from her resting spot, but then, most dragons are not called until their Fae companions have entered their second or third century.

Now that I've been conscripted into the FGA, I'm wondering if I'll ever be able to call her. There are very few Dragonblades left in the world and it would be a shame if this Dragon never came to my call.

Thinking about my Dragon keeps my thoughts away from the separation to come.

"How're you doing, Mari?" Dorian murmurs.

I shrug. What can I say?

Dorian's Dragonblade mark rests between his shoulder blades. I've always thought it was a bit of bad luck to have mine so prominently displayed. How could I be a successful assassin, thief or spy if I could be outed as a Dragonblade the moment someone saw me?

Now I realize it's doubly inconvenient. There will be no flying incognito at the FGA.

Even if the other students don't realize how very inappropriate this placement is for me personally, they will still know that I don't belong.

"We can run," Dorian offers. "Just take off, make our own way in the world."

I blink back tears and give a watery chuckle. "Oh, Dorian, don't be ridiculous. If we ran away, I wouldn't be able to wreak havoc at the FGA. They have no idea what they're in for."

Dorian lets out a bark of laughter. "That's right, cousin, and don't you forget it. You're going to do just fine. It's the rest of the world who needs to watch out."

Gabriel steps over and bumps Dorian out of the way, slinging an arm around my shoulders. "Which FaeGuard do you think will come first?"

"With any luck, the one that results in the least amount of embarrassment for me."

"Aw, Mari," Malia slides into my other side, hooking an arm around my waist.

"It's going to be okay," I tell them both, even as I worry about Gabriel's question.

There's really no anticipating the order of the Guards and I can't decide which would be worse: for the FGA to arrive first or for them to arrive last.

Apparently, though, I should have been worrying about when The Guard for the High Crimes Academy would arrive. As luck would have it, they arrived first, shaking the ground with the impact of their steeds' thundering hooves.

Taking a deep breath for courage, I walk through the crowds with the twins and my cousins, choking back tears.

We reach the edge of the clearing where the Guard is waiting and quickly say our goodbyes.

"I'll write," Malia whispers in my ear. "You have your mirrors, right?"

"Of course. Be safe, Malia."

She steps back and Blade steps forward. He's grown so much this year. He's now taller than me and I take comfort in knowing how strong he is, how strong they both are.

He hugs me and says back to me the words I said to Malia. "Stay safe, Mari."

I grin. "You too."

Dorian and Gabriel both hug me tight and promise to stay in touch.

I then watch as they join other student Criminals in mounting horses provided by the Guard.

Th Guard surrounds them a moment later. and they take off at a swift gallop.

I blink and they're gone.

A surge in sound rises at my back as people realize one of the Dragonblades is still present.

Moments later, the guard for another Academy arrives and more students say their goodbyes, mount horses and disappear into the distance.

Four more Travel Guards arrive and depart before finally the Guard for the FGA appears.

The rider at the front has a banner with all of True Love's symbols emblazoned across it.

Two doves, each with a wedding ring in its beak face each other over an intricately designed heart.

Interlocking scrollwork runs along the edges of the banner, two unending lines that continually cross paths, then break apart only to come back together once more.

All of it together—the doves with symbols of love in their beaks, the heart of unbroken lines and the scrollwork of interconnected ones —represent the enduring nature of love.

I roll my eyes at the sight.

I have no idea how I'm going to survive this placement.

I've spent my entire life in weapons training and stealth maneuvers and now I'm being sent to The Love Academy.

I heave a sigh.

There's no avoiding it and as I have no one left to say goodbye to, I might as well get it over with.

I sling my backpack over my shoulder, grab my additional two bags and walk forward.

Murmurs rise at my back again, as everyone realizes a Dragonblade is about to enter the FGA.

History in the making.

I avoid eye contact with everyone as I show my letter to the first Guardsman I encounter. He doesn't even blink an eye at the mark on my cheek, just checks my letter, gives me a nod and directs me to a gorgeous steed the color of wheat.

"What's his name?"

"Bladerunner."

As ridiculous as it is, the horse's name releases some of my tension.

"Well, Bladerunner," I say to him. "I can't think of a better name for a Dragonblade's steed, so I am very happy to be your partner on this journey." I stroke a hand down his snout.

Remembering the carrot I had stored in the pocket of my backpack for just this moment, I fish it out and offer it to Bladerunner.

He happily accepts and while he's chomping away, I get to work securing my two bags to his back.

Still avoiding eye contact with the other students who have started to arrive and are making friends with their assigned steeds, I pull myself onto Bladerunner's back, then lean forward to murmur in his ear.

"Are you serious right now?" Someone close to me exclaims.

So here's the deal.

The Fae are blessed with many gifts. Some are more curses than gifts, but still they're gifts.

And one of those is beauty.

Every manner of Fae, from brownies to nymphs to trolls to High Fae, have the gift of glamour.

It's true that beauty is in the eye of the beholder, which means that someone beautiful to me could be hideous to someone else.

Glamour, however, changes all of that.

We can use glamour to conceal ourselves, to change our appearances and to cloak ourselves in beauty. When we do the latter, we appear beautiful to all of the non-Fae creatures of the many realms. They see their own perception of beauty.

So knowing that, I find it exceptionally unfair when certain Fae are also gifted with a natural beauty, one so vibrant that they are wondrous, incandescent and radiant to look upon.

The Shining Ones.

This sneering man-boy confronting me *isn't* a shining one.

But he's pretty epically close.

And unfortunately, the sneer on his face and the scorn in his voice, do nothing to detract from his beauty.

Tall and built, he has thick, tightly cropped black hair, beautiful dark skin, piercing Fae green eyes, strong facial features and a voice just deep enough to send a shiver down my back.

"Excuse me?" I mostly say this to give me time to recover from almost swallowing my tongue when I first catch sight of him.

"You're wearing the mark of a Dragonblade."

I raise an eyebrow. "Congratulations. You've succeeded in stating the obvious." I'm pretty impressed at my ability to pull out the snark when I'm fighting back the drool, but honestly, his attitude is helping a lot with that.

"Dragonblades do not belong at the FGA."

"I have a letter indicating otherwise."

He scoffs. "Let me see that letter."

"Uh, no. I've already shown it to the Guard. You have no authority here. Go away."

He lets out a growl and for a minute I think he might try and knock me off my steed, but then one of the FaeGuards lets out a piercing whistle and we're off.

It's a hard and brutal ride, but also quite exhilarating.

Bladerunner is an incredible steed. He has speed and agility and riding him is like flying.

As we move through the landscape, I try to peek through the shield the Guard has erected around us, but it's no use.

The shield's perfect in every way.

It's a bit of complicated magic the Guard uses to keep the location of each Academy secret. Even attendees of the Academies never know their true locations.

By the time we arrive at our destination, night has fallen.

The moon is full and bright overhead and shines down on the Fae Godparent Academy.

I've never really paid much attention to talk of the other Academies, mostly because I only ever expected to attend the HCA.

This is why I'm stunned at my first glimpse of the FGA. It's not your typical academy building. It has turrets and towers, battlements and arrow loops, a portcullis, drawbridge and a freaking moat.

Apparently, I'll be living in a castle while attending the Fae Godparent Academy. Who knew?

Chapter Four

THE NEXT COUPLE of hours pass in a whirlwind.

I barely have a chance to give Bladerunner a pat goodbye before we're ushered into the castle, down a long hall and into a giant room where we're divided into lines according to our last names.

I step into the line labeled D-F and wait my turn.

As I get closer, I begin to hear the conversations taking place as the students check in.

There appear to be three women handling registration.

The first woman checks the students' names off a list.

The students then receive a large envelope from the second woman and a smaller one from the third.

As the students walk away, I'm able to catch a glimpse of what's inside the larger envelope (a stack of papers from what I can tell) but I have no idea what the smaller envelope contains.

Finally, it's my turn. I step forward, prepared to provide my name when the woman asks, but she takes one look at my mark, checks me off a list and motions me to move along.

I move to the second woman at the table and she grabs an envelope that's set off to one side, separate from the rest of them.

It's labeled Marigold Dragonblade.

A quick glance down reassures me that this isn't unusual as all the envelopes on the table have names on them.

The woman holds my envelope out to me, but when I go to take it, she maintains a firm grip. "This envelope has absolutely critical information inside it. Do not lose it, do not let it out of your sight. Read it carefully and as soon as possible, but not right this moment, not here." She then lets go of the envelope and motions to the next student in line.

I move down the table and accept a small, lumpy envelope from the third woman. She has nothing to say to me, so I step away from the table, but loiter in the area.

I make a production of peeking inside the smaller envelope (it has a key inside it). Really, though, I'm just trying to listen to the conversations the second woman is having with other students.

Over and over again, I hear her say the words, "Critical information," but not once do I hear admonishments about not losing said information.

What I do hear, however, not just from the second woman, but from the first and the third as well, are friendly greetings welcoming the students to the Fae Godparent Academy.

I roll my eyes.

If they think not speaking to me or refusing to welcome me to the Academy is going to hurt my feelings, well, they've clearly never met a

Criminal before.

And I don't care what anyone says.

Assessment results or not, I'll always be a Criminal at heart.

I glance around and realize a lot of the students are lingering and staring.

Wonderful.

Time to move on.

I open the smaller envelope and extract an old fashioned key, along with a card that says, "Aphrodite's Wing, Mother Tower, Room 276."

Great.

I move through the crowds of students, who part for me silently, and return to the hallway where I find the students who rode in with me from Shadowstorm Waystation waiting.

"Finally," a girl with long, blonde hair exclaims.

I raise an eyebrow and stare her down.

"Now, Brittany." The jerk from earlier sets a hand on her shoulder and gives me what I'm coming to recognize as his signature sneer. "We shouldn't expect the *Criminal* to understand how things are done around here. We'll just have to educate her, I guess."

Brittany smirks at me. "Good point, Finn. You see, Dragonblade —"

"Let me interrupt you right there," I say. "I'm not interested in how things are *done around here*." I make quote marks in the air around those last three words. "Frankly, that would make me both predictable and boring, and I'm way too interesting to ever become one of those."

I blow past the two of them and stride toward the stairs I noted when we first came in.

"Hey, where are you going?" Brittany exclaims. "Mark here is supposed to be giving us a tour."

I turn from the third stair up and look down at the lot of them. "Which one of you is Mark?"

"Uh, that's me." A dark-haired older student steps forward. "They ask the upper years to show the new students where their rooms are and such."

"So, the tour you're taking us on is to our rooms?"

"Yes."

I chuckle. "I'm pretty sure I can follow the signs." I sling a careless hand to the one beside me that proclaims, "Aphrodite's Wing," with an arrow pointing up the stairs. I then turn and run up them.

I hear Brittany exclaim behind me, "What an idiot! Those signs are sure to get her lost."

As if a Criminal could ever get lost anywhere, even when inside a foreign Academy.

I follow the relevant signs, ignoring the ones that have clearly been hung for misdirection purposes only, and within moments, I'm standing in a giant circular room with three doors opposite me.

The doors are labeled Mothers, Fathers and Neutrals.

I let out a giant sigh.

I kind of want to go to the Neutral door out of sheer annoyance at being labeled a Mother.

I find it highly offensive given I never wanted to be a parent in the first place and now I have to play the part of Mother to a bunch of people who have been deluded into hoping for love.

I'm already disgusted and the year has barely begun.

I stalk across the room, ignoring the silent, staring students who are lounging on chairs and couches, and fling open the door labeled

Mothers, revealing more stairs leading up to what might be a tower of some sort.

The door behind me opens and Brittany's voice follows me up the stairs. "How in all the magical realms did she get here so quickly?"

"Well, she is a Criminal, you know," I hear Finn reply. "She's probably stolen the blueprints to the place."

"Jerk," I mutter as I reach the top of the stairs and find myself in another circular room, facing three hallways, one directly ahead and two on either side of me.

I smirk, then turn and holler down the stairs, "Criminal's not a bad word, you know. In fact, it's about the nicest compliment I could give you. Shame none of you qualify."

Without waiting for a reply, I head for the hallway straight ahead. It's labeled rooms 100-149, but I'm fairly certain the sign's a lie.

Nothing new there.

The Fae specialize in lies.

The first room I encounter is labeled 252. I walk quickly, cataloguing the numbers as I go.

Even numbers on the left, odd numbers on the right.

274, 279—that's not right.

I step past 279 to confirm the next room is 278.

I spin around and note that directly across from 278 is 276, even though all the other doors on that side of the hall have odd numbers.

Right.

Do they think Criminals can't count?

How in the world would we have ever gotten so rich if that were the case?

A quickly muttered spell under my breath spins the six and nine into their proper positions.

I glance down at my key, wondering if it was spelled as well.

Holding it in the palm of my left hand, I slide my index finger down the shaft, coaxing the spell concealed upon its skin to reveal itself.

It takes a few moments, but eventually I can see the spell and the intended result once it's activated.

If used in any door other than the correct one, the key will explode in the user's hand.

It isn't a terribly harmful spell as the result would probably just be a singed hand and possibly a brand in the shape of a key, but otherwise, no lasting effects.

Too bad for them, these students have no idea who they're dealing with.

Time for a demonstration of a Criminal's power.

I continue to handle the key, turning it over and over in my hand, getting a feel for the spell soaked into its skin.

I'll definitely recognize the magic if I ever encounter it again.

Carefully manipulating the spell, I draw it away from the key and expand it slowly, ever so slowly.

I don't want it to pop too soon.

As I weave the spell, drawing it out, I listen for the sound of footsteps.

I have no idea why none of the students have arrived yet to check out their rooms or even to watch me try to enter the wrong one.

There has to be more I'm not quite understanding yet.

Perhaps this spell is just a distraction and the real spell is still waiting to activate.

With this in mind, I adjust the parameters minutely.

Another beat to wait and listen, then when I gauge the timing is right, I release the spell.

Chapter Five

IT'S CLEAR IN my first few hours at the FGA, I'm not making friends left and right.

At meals, we're required to sit at our year's table, which means I'm stuck eating my meal with all the students who arrived on horseback with me, including Finn and Brittany.

Brittany's fuming from the results of my spell, undoubtedly furious because I either outsmarted her or because she was an unwitting victim of someone else's machinations.

As all the Year Ones arrived at the same moment I did, it would be easy to discount their participation in this first obnoxious prank.

In fact, it's tempting to assume it was perpetrated by some upper years, in what amounts to a bit of hazing.

However, I'm suspicious by nature, so pretty much everyone, including teachers at the Academy, are suspects.

"How did you do that?" The girl sitting across the table from me asks.

She has spiky black hair and appears to be intrigued, rather than scared or annoyed.

"Seriously. How did you take that spell and turn it around like that? That's upper-level stuff."

I shrug.

"My name's Lia, by the way."

"Mari."

"Can you show me how to do that? How to manipulate someone else's magic so it works for you rather than against you?"

Before I can answer, the boy sitting next to her leans forward, a lock of brown hair falling into his eyes. "I want in on this too. I'm Max. From what my older brothers tell me, some of the students around here are pretty hard core with their pranks. Knowing how to reveal spells and turn them back on the wielder would be priceless here."

"So can you?" Lia pushes.

"Probably not." I shake my head.

She looks crestfallen. "Well, why not?"

"Yeah, why not?" Max demands.

I shrug. "I'm a Dragonblade. I've been training for this kind of thing my whole life. Only I trained to counteract assassination and kidnapping spells, not silly little hazing ones."

"No wonder your spell was so powerful," Lia muttered.

I grin, remembering the way all the doors on the second floor had exploded open at the same time, including my own.

I could have kept my door outside the bubble of the spell, but instead, due to a highly suspicious nature (it's the Criminal in me), I allowed the spell full reign, though not before taking refuge along the wall between my door and the one next to it, of course.

Turns out I was right to be suspicious. When my door had flown open, an absolute torrent of blue dye had exploded from it, shooting straight across the hall into room 277.

The best part was when I discovered that room belonged to Brittany. Listening to her screech about the mess was music to my ears.

Although it kind of sucks we're right across the hall from each other.

"I heard the spell disintegrated all the locks," Max says. "Is that true?"

"Oh, it's true," Lia says. "And while everyone else was freaking out, she just calmly replaced her own locks."

"You brought your own locks?" Max exclaims.

"I'm a Criminal," I remind him.

"Oh, right." He nods sagely.

I'm not sure he really understands, but I'm not going to explain that the locks on my door were never going to remain in place.

No Criminal worthy of their magic would ever sleep behind an unsecured door, and by unsecured, I mean featuring any lock series not produced by a Criminal organization.

So while the other students have to wait for new locks to be supplied by the Academy, I've already replaced mine and added two others besides.

Good luck to anyone, employee of the Academy or student, who tries to get past my locks. Locks produced by Criminals always have a built-in punishment feature.

I smirk down at my soup, anticipating the first time one of the bullies in my wing tries to break in anyway.

It'll only happen once. Of that, I'm absolutely positive.

"Maybe you can teach us something small," Lia suggests.

"Great idea," Max exclaims.

I can't believe they're still harping on this. On the other hand, if these two are sincere, and my instincts say they are, having a couple friends might make this entire experience less torturous.

"I suppose we can give it a try."

"Awesome! So what grouping are you in?" Lia asks.

I just stare at her.

"You did open the big envelope, didn't you?" Max says.

"Not yet."

"We're all first years," Lia says, "so we'll be taking the same classes, but there are five different groupings. Max and I are in A together, so we have the same schedule."

"I'm quite looking forward to Spellcasting," Max says. "We're supposed to learn an awful lot this first year. Though it might be a bit boring for you, Mari."

"Well, if they're teaching us how to make people fall in love, that'll be new for me." I roll my eyes.

Max and Lia just stare at me.

"What?"

"You can't *make* people fall in love," Lia says.

"Yeah, that would be wrong," Max says.

I raise an eyebrow. I'm beginning to see why no Criminal has been conscripted to the FGA before me. Right vs. wrong isn't exactly something we tend to worry about.

"It'd be a complete abuse of our powers," Lia says. "We're supposed to make true matches, help the right people find each other.

The more love in the world, the better, right?"

Are they being serious, right now? "Do you honestly believe that?"

"What?" they chorus.

I look around quickly, then lean forward to hiss softly, "That the Throne isn't demanding certain matches be made for the good of the Fae."

Lia and Max both rear back, glance at each other, then back at me.

They move in such harmony, it reminds me of the twins and gives me a pang of homesickness.

"Are you two related?" I demand suspiciously.

They look at each other, then burst into laughter.

"No," Lia giggles. "We're just best friends."

"Yeah, our mums grew up together and built houses right next door to each other. We've known each other all our lives and I guess we're a lot alike at this point," Max says.

"I'll say," I mutter.

"Anyway, back to the subject of matchmaking," Lia says. "The Fae Godparenting Act protects all godparents from interference. We're pure, perhaps the only pure profession left in Faerie. The Throne is specifically forbidden from interfering in our matches."

"You'll see," Max says. "They'll probably cover all of that in History of Matchmaking."

"Or Politics," Lia says.

"Maybe both," they chorus together.

Unbelievable. They're so naive. I can't believe they actually think a simple decree would neuter the Throne. "If you say so." Who am I to disabuse them of their starry-eyed vision of True Love? I've no doubt they'll learn soon enough that happily ever after is just a myth and that the Throne has its tentacles everywhere.

We exchange our mirror codes and when I get back to my room, I message both Lia and Max the good news that I'm also in Grouping A.

Unfortunately, there's a downside to that news, which I discover the next morning, when I arrive at our first class, Spellcasting 101, and discover Brittany and Finn are in that Grouping as well.

Even worse, it's assigned seating and I'm sharing a table with Finn.

"Look to the person sitting beside you," Professor Lionell announces from the front of the class.

I glance at Finn from the corner of my eye, but he's staring straight ahead, back rigidly straight.

Clearly he's as happy as me to be sharing this table.

"This person," Professor Lionell says, "is critical to your success here at the FGA."

Wonderful.

"The two of you have been chosen to work together as lab and study partners *for the year*. These partnerships were chosen based upon your Assessment results. There is no disputing these partnerships. They are set in stone. If you do not like the person you are working with," she pauses to glare around the room, "*get over it.*"

A couple nervous twitters spill from some of the other students.

Right.

Easy for them to laugh.

They probably like their partners.

In fact, right in front of us, Max and Lia are partnered together. Perhaps, given how close they are, it isn't surprising their results landed them together. Still, it isn't exactly fair, now is it?

"You and your partner will work together this year, and depending upon the results of your end-of-year assessments, you may in fact, find yourselves partnered for the entire tenure of your time here at the FGA."

I might have to stab myself in the eye if that horrifying possibility comes to pass.

Or perhaps I'll just stab Finn instead.

"Your marks in this class and indeed, in all of your classes, and your ability to progress to the next level at this Academy are all dependent upon your ability to work with your partner to create incandescent matches of love." She flings out her arms in a bit of melodrama as she pronounces those final words.

I feel nauseous.

I'm not sure if it's the bandying about of the word love or if it's the thought of having to work with the pompous, arrogant, judgmental, hotter–than–hot Finn.

Probably a bit of both.

"Let's get on with it, shall we? Open the mirrors at your spot, find our class homepage and complete the survey located there. You have exactly ten minutes."

I'm relieved to note the mirror is the exact same I'm used to working with at home.

It's embedded in our table. When not activated, it blends in with the rest of the table.

However, if you know what you're looking for, you can pick out the mirrors from the slight discoloration around the edges of each. There a large one one directly in front of me and another in front of Finn.

A quick press of my thumb in the slight indent located at the top left corner of the table wakes my mirror up.

Finn does the same in the top right corner of the table.

Both mirrors come online, lifting up and away from the table, so that they're standing upright directly in front of us.

For one brief moment, I'm looking at myself in the mirror, then my reflection fades away to a black screen with the words, "Welcome, Mari."

Out of the corner of my eye, I can see Finn's mirror welcoming him.

I touch the screen and the words disappear, revealing five icons labeled "History of Matchmaking," "Politics of Matchmaking," "History of Fae Magic," "Spellcasting 101," and "Matchmaking 101."

The nausea is now joined by a terrible sinking sensation in my stomach.

I've spent my entire life preparing for coursework like, "Weaponry and Spellcasting," "Fae-Induced Wars and Other Historical Events," and "Fae Magic for Stealth and Infiltration."

How in the world am I going to experience success at something as ridiculous as Matchmaking 101?

One step at a time.

I can't afford to panic now.

A quick glance at Finn's screen and I can see's he's already deep into the survey.

I touch the icon labeled "Spellcasting 101" and the screen jumps to the homepage for the class. There's a swirl of green smoke and when it dissipates, a survey is waiting for me.

A quick scan of the questions and I realize they're just to find out what my background is in spell casting. It's a typical pre-test to determine what the students know and don't know.

I hesitate, uncertain if I should be brutally honest or not.

As if Professor Lionell can read my thoughts, she says, "It's important you're completely honest in your answers. If you're not honest, we cannot help you grow into your powers. Dig deep, find your truth and own it. Share what you know. Share what you do not know. Share what you hope to learn. This is the only way you'll ever reach your full potential and the only way your matches will be truly *incandescent*."

Whatever.

Still it's a good point, so I start answering the questions truthfully.

To a point.

I have no intention of giving away any Criminal secrets.

When I reach the end of the survey, I hesitate only a moment before pressing the submit button.

A few moments later, the professor announces, "Time's up. If you will refresh your screen, you will notice that your partner's survey has been delivered to your inbox."

I inhale sharply amid the gasps that resound around the room.

"Oh, didn't I mention it? Yes, in order to work well with each other, it is important that you understand each other's strengths *and* weaknesses. These survey results are entirely private, not to be shared with any other students. You will protect your partner's information as you would your own. You have five minutes to read over your partner's answers before we discuss them."

I avoid looking at Finn as I quickly refresh the mirror's screen and pull up his survey from my inbox.

A quick scan of his answers tells me exactly why we've been

partnered together.

Like me, Finn comes from an ancient line. In his case, all of his ancestors were Fae Godparents as opposed to Fae Criminals, but otherwise, his history reads much like my own.

He spent his entire life training to become a Fae Godparent, learning spells to manipulate events and people, to bring together the perfect set of circumstances to ensure a stable match.

Interesting that he doesn't mention love once in his answers.

I'm thinking Finn has a more realistic view of what Fae Godparents are accomplishing in the world than Lia and Max.

"All right, then. You've had enough time to get a sense of your partner's background. Now, I want you to turn and have a discussion. Ask your partner questions. You'll note that the survey didn't ask for your philosophy around matchmaking or true love, as it is assumed by the powers-that-be that you would never have been identified for this Academy if you didn't truly believe in the mission of happily ever afters. Having said that, though, there's a lot of room in there for how that mission is achieved, so go ahead and discuss where you stand on each of these issues. You have fifteen minutes to get to know each other better and then you'll be introducing your partner to the class."

The Throne of the Fae has cursed me.

I just know it.

"Right." Finn spins on his stool to face me. "You don't belong here, it's perfectly obvious, but I'm not failing because of some nefarious, Criminal plot. So let's hear it. What in all of the Fae are you doing here?"

Chapter Six

UGH. THERE MUST be something seriously wrong with me that I find this idiot attractive.

Why can't his appearance match his personality?

"I'm here for the same reason you are," I tell him. "The Assessment."

"There's no way you're a legitimate placement here, not with that birthmark."

I raise an eyebrow. "Just because it's never happened before doesn't mean I don't belong."

"Do you even believe in True Love?"

"Do you?"

He looks surprised. "Of course I do. I'm here, aren't I?"

"And yet, you think I don't?"

"You're a Criminal."

"And Criminals can't fall in love?" I'm not sure why I'm arguing the point.

Okay, yes, I do.

I hate him and that's why.

"Name one."

"Bonnie and Clyde."

"They were human."

"Are you sure of that?"

He gets an arrested look on his face and I smirk at him.

He scowls. "Oh, come on. Stop messing with me. They were human and so they don't count."

"They were Criminals, so I say they do."

"Fine. Then name me two *Fae* Criminals."

"Give me a break. Most Criminals would never admit to feeling any sort of emotion at all. It just gives others ammunition against them. But if you insist, my mother went a bit insane when my father died. She still mourns him to this day. So yes, there *are* Criminals who have fallen in love."

Now, did I think he loved her in return as much as she loved him? Of course not, but I wasn't going to say that, for it would ruin my argument. The truth is I never met my father so maybe he *did* love her, but that was highly doubtful. After all, he'd spent the majority of their centuries together causing wars in foreign lands. When he died, despite having given him many sons, my mother had already spent most of her lifetime alone (and by most, I mean entire centuries). No, my father did *not* love my mother, certainly not to the degree that she loved him.

And that, you see, is why I do not believe in True Love, and why I'm quite possibly the worst candidate ever to enroll at this Academy.

"You have five minutes left. Be sure you know exactly what you're going to share about your partner," Professor Lionell calls out.

Great.

"So you do believe in True Love then?" Finn says.

I make a face. "I believe in political machinations and delusions of happily ever afters. If you want to call it True Love, well, I can't stop you. It's all semantics anyway."

He groans. "That attitude is not going to help us make any matches this year."

"Of course, it will. A good dose of reality is critical to success when setting any goals. Delusions will only get you so far."

"Whatever."

"All right, class. Time for introductions. We'll start up here with Ainsley and Brittany."

It takes heroic effort, but I manage not to roll my eyes. Of course, we get to hear from Brittany first.

The dark-haired Fae sitting at Brittany's side stands and faces the class. "This is Brittany Fairweather. She has five Fae godparents in her ancestry, dating all the way back to the matching of Queen Cleopatra and Marcus Antonius."

Murmurs roll around the room.

I lose the battle and roll my eyes after all. It's not like she said Brittany's family had actually achieved that match, just that they were Godparents in that timeframe.

Actually, no one knows who made that match. It's a highly guarded Fae secret, but even without knowing who made it, we all know it was a Fae-orchestrated match, which means the war that followed was Fae-orchestrated as well.

How anyone can believe the Throne of Faerie isn't involved when the Fae maneuver matches such as that one, I have no idea.

Brittany goes next, introducing Ainsley as a Heartsleeve (even I've heard the name, though I've no clue what matches they claim).

Lia leans back and whispers to me, "Watch out for Ainsley. From what I understand, her family has ruled this school for centuries. She intends to keep that mantel of power, I'm sure."

Based on the smug look on Ainsley's face as Brittany drones on and on about her pedigree—seventeen Fae Godparents in her line, blah-blah-blah—I'd have to agree.

The introductions continue that way down the row, then switching to our side of the room, starting at the front again and working its way back toward us.

Max and Lia introduce each other with a bit of humor and a couple funny stories from growing up together. Neither one mentions any ancestors or their pedigrees.

I knew there was a reason I liked them.

We're the last table to present.

Professor Lionell gives me a nod, so I stand and say, "This is Finn Heartstone. He apparently comes from an extraordinarily long line of Fae Godparents, which I'm sure is quite impressive." I pause for a beat. "To some of us anyway. He's a credit to the Academy, I'm sure, since he's bought all the propaganda around True Love and all of that." I make eye contact with Professor Lionell. "I'm sure he will make *incandescent* matches for the *Throne*." I place particular emphasis on that final word as I settle back in my seat.

A beat of silence follows as Professor Lionell raises an eyebrow and continues to maintain eye contact.

If she thinks I'm looking away first, she's not at all aware of who has been invited to the table this year.

Finally, she shifts her gaze to Finn and gives him the nod.

Finn stands and says, "I'm sure she needs no introductions, but this is Marigold Dragonblade."

"Mari," I interrupt to say.

Finn gives a short nod and continues, "Mari comes from a very long and probably equally impressive line of Criminals. She's the first in her family to be a Godparent and I know we're all quite curious to see what kind of matches she will make. With her cynicism and lack of belief in True Love, we may be looking at an entirely new wave of matchmaking."

"Or perhaps simply the blinders will be lifted and we'll all see the matches for what they truly are," I say.

"And what might that be, Mari?" Professor Lionell asks.

"Political machinations at their best." I pause for one tiny sliver of a second, wondering if I dare say what I'm thinking.

Ah, well.

Who am I kidding?

"Weapons of the Fae at their worst."

I honestly can't help myself. It's the Criminal in me. We simply are *not* shy about expressing our opinions.

We say what we mean and we definitely mean what we say.

Luckily, Professor Lionell doesn't seem to mind my outspokenness. "I think that's a lovely segue into our mission statement. We've heard two very distinct camps around the ideology of matchmaking. One camp believes the Fae should focus on making matches that benefit Faerie. The other camp believes that True Love must prevail and that a happily ever after should always be the end goal, regardless of whether a particular match will benefit or harm the Fae. So. Let's get to it."

What follows is a passionate and lively debate about the two ideologies, and I must say, I find myself quite enjoying it.

I'm not even put out that Max and Lia are firmly on the side of True Love while I'm pretty much all by myself on the political machinations side.

Even those who see my point still feel there's some happy medium where True Love can be manipulated to benefit the Fae and all of Faerie.

Finn happens to be somewhere in that gray area in the middle even though he does a good job pretending to be on True Love's side.

I can tell that most of the students are buying his passionate defense of the "power of love," but I call hogwash on that. I read his survey answers, so I know the truth.

All in all, it ends up being a very interesting first class and I'm actually starting to think the FGA might not be so bad after all.

Our next class is Politics of Matchmaking, which is also pretty interesting and gives me many opportunities to point out the political ramifications of certain matches the Fae have sponsored.

I can see on some of the students' faces that the bubble may be cracking just a little.

By the end of that class, I'm worried that Max and Lia may never speak to me again, but they link arms with me the minute the bell rings and drag me to the cafeteria to grab a lunch, then to the courtyard to eat.

I guess they don't mind my cynicism.

After lunch, we have History of Fae Magic, during which I get into a debate with Finn about whether the infamous Fae spell that concealed the city of Atlantis was a bit of matchmaking gone awry.

This is one of the most contested events in Fae history. Atlantis disappeared right after a trio of Fae arrived in the city: a Criminal and two Fae Godparents.

No one has seen them or the city of Atlantis since.

The prevailing theory among most factions of Faerie is that the Criminal was somehow responsible for unleashing a terrible fate upon Atlantis and all of its residents.

It's a ridiculous theory, of course. A much more probable one is that the Fae godparents made the wrong match.

They may not want to believe it, but all evidence throughout history pretty much proves that Criminal Fae are adept at stealth and secrecy. No one ever suspects they were involved in whatever comes about.

Whereas, Fae godparents have a well-earned reputation of screwing things up with the absolute worst matches in history.

Just look at the terrible mess they made of things by matching Helen of Sparta not once, but twice, and the second time while she was still married.

Yeah. I'm sure they were going for a True Love match both times.

If that's the case, have I mentioned that I've got a bit of land for sale in the Faerie Wylding Forests?

I pretty much say as much in class, causing a bit of laughter and I'm pretty sure, pulling a few more students over to my side of the True Love vs. Political Machinations debate.

Finn just glares and mutters under his breath, "Criminal brat."

I raise an eyebrow.

If he wants to insult me, well, he's going to have to try harder than that.

In History of Matchmaking, we debate which match had the most political ramifications: the one between Lucifer and the demoness Galvidriana or the one between the fallen angel Neruna and the alpha wolf of the enormous Herazidah pack.

Both changed history.

One, however, changed the entire landscape of hell for all of its denizens, so clearly the match between Lucifer and Galvidriana was more impactful.

Finn is stubborn, though, to say the least and definitely hates being wrong.

He keeps making the most ridiculous arguments about the ways in which packs are now governed and how those traditions can be traced all the way back to Neruna's influence.

Whatever.

He makes me insane.

By the time we make it to our last class of the day, Matchmaking 101, I'm ready to go through with it.

I just need a knife and for Finn to stand still for ten seconds tops.

Too bad I left all my weapons in my room.

Then, as if things aren't bad enough, they get infinitely worse.

We're barely seated in our chairs before Professor Halloran is ruining my good mood and with it, the entire school year.

"You'll be working quite closely with your partners all year long. If you were not already planning to spend every minute of your free time together, well, *you certainly are now.*"

He can't possibly be serious.

"You will need more time than you think to plan and strategize exactly how you will manage to accomplish the most exquisite of matches this year."

What is it with these professors expecting *exquisite incandescence* from their first years?

"You might as well give up any thought of having free time or fun little jaunts into the other realms. You'll be working every minute you're awake here at the Academy *and*, other than during school-approved holidays, you'll be working anytime you leave the Academy grounds as well."

I did *not* sign up for this.

"This year, your matches will all be human. These will be the easiest matches you will make during your time here at the FGA. Next year—*if* you make it that far—you'll be leveled up and all your matches will be shifters."

"Shouldn't shifter matches be easier than human ones?" One of the other students, I think her name is Petra, asks.

"Yeah, they don't even need us," Max says. "They already have mates."

"Yes, yes, good question," Halloran says. "Except shifter mates are notoriously difficult to find. Think about it. Their one true mate could be anywhere in the world. How do they find each other?"

"The same way humans find each other?" Lia offers.

"And how do they do that?" Professor Halloran asks.

"They go on dates?" Brittany asks.

"And how do they find these dates?"

Silence.

"The Fae help them, of course," Professor Halloran exclaims. "So, yes, in some ways, matching shifters can be a lot easier than matching humans. Once we manage to get the two shifters into the same space at one time, they usually recognize each other and things progress from there.

"However, shifters are also notoriously stubborn. If for some reason, mates fail to recognize each other when they first meet, it becomes increasingly less likely they will ever recognize each other.

"This is where we come in. We have to somehow smooth things out and help the shifters recognize each other before their bond dies. So that will be your second year. Working with shifter mates who have already met, but are in danger of never mating."

Great. That doesn't sound difficult at all.

"Your third year, your matches will be vampires and your fourth year, you'll be ready for the demons."

That sounds kind of fun.

"But let's not get ahead of ourselves. Today we're going to focus on your matches for this year. They've already been chosen for you. You will work with your partner to ensure these matches happen and that all the individuals assigned to the two of you live happily ever after."

Gross.

"You will note that some of the individuals you've been assigned already have their matches identified, so all you have to do is figure out how to help them fall in love."

Unbelievable. They've already decided who should be together. I have no idea how anyone can sit through these classes and not believe these matches are being manipulated for the good of someone else.

"Some of your individuals, however, have no matches assigned as of yet. In these cases, you have some flexibility and should focus on finding the perfect match for your individual."

So at least some of our targets will have a chance of falling in love, rather than being manipulated into it.

Oh, who am I kidding?

It's all about the manipulation, whether someone higher up than us decides who they're going to be with or whether we do that ourselves.

"If you open your mirrors, you will find in your inbox all the details of the individuals you will match this semester. You have fifteen minutes to review the materials, then you'll be discussing with your partner strategies for making these matches a reality."

I activate my mirror and pull up my inbox.

A message labeled "Assigned Matches" is on top.

I open it.

Marigold Dragonblade:

Match Papers for the following individuals are attached:

Adriana Charming
Adam Charming
Victor Charming
Lyle Charming
Steven Brighton
Bethany Brighton
Harriet Brighton
Cinderella

Study each carefully. Your marks in this course depend upon your partnership with Finn Heartstone. In order to advance in the Academy, the two of you must successfully complete a happily–ever–after match for each of the above individuals.

Sincerely,

The Fae Godparent Academy Board

Chapter Seven

THE MINUTE CLASS is over, I escape as quickly as possible, ignoring Finn's demand that we get together that evening to work out a strategy.

We just spent the last forty-five minutes arguing about the matches we've been given and I'm not looking forward to spending the evening on repeat.

He yells something after me as I bolt out of the classroom.

Five minutes later, I'm lying across my bed, arm slung over my eyes, trying to stop myself from obsessing over all the sniping Finn subjected me to throughout the day, class after class.

I fail miserably.

Obsessing has commenced.

Then I'm saved by a knock on the door.

The knife under my pillow is in my hand, almost without thought.

I'd like to think I don't need the knife here at the FGA, but I actually think I might need it more than when I was surrounded by

Criminals every day of my life.

Holding it down at my side, I walk to the door and stand to one side of it. "Who is it?"

"It's Lia and Max."

"Just a minute."

I'm barefoot so I can't hide the knife in my boot like I usually do so I turn and fling it at the cork board on the opposite side of the room.

It stabs deep.

I wince.

Pretty sure that went straight into the wall.

Oh, well.

That's what they get for bringing a Criminal into their midst.

I unlock my three deadbolts, remove the chain and swing open the door.

"Wow." Lia pushes her way inside, Max on her heels.

I shut the door behind them and Lia examines my locks.

"Overkill much?" She asks.

"You wouldn't think so if you were a Criminal out of your element, surrounded by potential enemies."

Max grins. "Finn's getting on your last nerve, isn't he?"

I shrug. "He's so stubborn."

"Yeah, we didn't get a whole lot done because you guys were more entertaining," Lia admits.

"I don't see how." I head back across the room, grabbing my knife and yanking it free as I go.

The corkboard and a piece of the wall come with it.

I let out a grunt of annoyance, then set the corkboard down on the desk, settle my hand against it firmly and give the knife a good yank.

It comes free, leaving a nice rip in the cork and—I glance up—a fairly decent-sized hole in the wall.

Oh, well.

I set the knife down and turn to face Lia and Max, who have settled on the bed and are staring at me, wide-eyed.

"What?"

Lia shakes her head. "Nothing. Have you heard about Ainsley yet?"

I glance at the mirror over my dresser, then calculate how much time has passed. "It's only been an hour since class let out. How can something have happened already?"

"Oh, nothing happened, per se," Max says, "but she's definitely on the warpath."

"About what?"

"Apparently she expected to be partnered with Finn herself."

"Well, she can have him. Wait. No, she can't. Not if it means I have to work with Brittany."

They both laugh.

"Then she found out who your matches are and she was really mad."

"Wait. How'd she find out that?"

Lia shrugs. "Finn must have told her."

"Well, what does it matter anyway?"

"Do you not know who you've been assigned to?" Max asks.

"Sure. A lot of Charmings and Brightons plus some woman named Cinderella, no last name."

"Well, the Charmings are the royal family of the Midnight Falls kingdom," Lia informs me, "and Aisling is absolutely livid that she hasn't been assigned the most influential matches of the season."

"Oh, please. I highly doubt the powers-that-be would trust a truly important match to a couple of Year Ones, especially when one of those is a Criminal."

"Ah-ah-ah." Max shakes his finger at me. "You're a Godparent now."

May the Throne of the Fae guide me.

At that moment, there comes another knock at the door, startling the three of us, and I realize I failed to reengage the locks.

In the next heartbeat, I'm on my feet, knife in hand, standing between the bed and the door. I plant my feet and demand, "Who is it?"

The door is flung open in response and Finn is standing there, arms crossed, glaring at me.

"Seriously?" I glare at him and brandish my knife. "That's an excellent way to get stabbed in the heart."

Lia and Max step up to either side of me in a show of loyalty and support I'll not soon forget.

Finn steps inside and closes the door behind him. "We're supposed to be working on our strategy. I'm not going to fail this course simply because you're too lazy to do the work."

I raise an eyebrow at him. "I'm not lazy. I simply refuse to beat my head against the wall needlessly, and by wall, I mean your refusal to admit when you're wrong."

"I am not wrong. There's a way we do matches around here and since you were born and raised a Criminal, you should absolutely defer to me in all things match-related."

I let out a hoot of laughter. "You go on thinking that, why don't you? And when you're willing to actually *listen* to my ideas, I'll consider spending my off-time in your presence. Otherwise, go away."

Instead of complying, he moves further into the room, grabs my office chair, swings it around and settles into it.

"So what are you three talking about? Have you figured out how you two are going to approach your matches?"

Lia and Max look at each other, then at me.

I throw up my hands in exasperation. "You might as well answer his question. He's too stubborn to leave until you do."

"Not really," Lia says hesitantly. "We're still debating options."

"Did any of them involve spying on your intended targets?"

"Sure," she replies. "We're planning to use our mirrors to catch a glimpse of their interactions with the people around them, see if there are any potential matches already in their vicinity."

"And did you discuss infiltrating your targets' households to spy on them in person? Did you discuss getting to know your targets personally so that you can better gauge who would be the right match for them?"

Lia looks at Max, who says, "We haven't discussed that, no, but it's an interesting idea, especially if we want to ensure it's a True Love match."

"It's not accepted policy for us to interact with our targets," Finn protests.

"If you don't interact with them, how on earth do you know whether the match is a good one or not?" I demand.

Lia and Max look stumped.

Finn just looks frustrated. "We just know, that's all, and if you were a true Godparent, you'd understand that."

I just smirk at him. "Well, I'm sorry if you don't like my Criminal mind, but when I commit to something, I insist on doing it right."

Finn rolls his eyes. "Fine. You write up your proposal and I'll write up mine and we'll compare them in class tomorrow. If Professor Halloran actually approves your plan, then fine, we'll do it your way. But I'll be very surprised if he does." He stands and heads for the door, pausing there to add grudgingly, "See you at dinner."

Lia whirls on me the minute the door is closed. "He's so into you, it's not even funny."

"Have you lost your mind? He hates me."

"Lia's right," Max says. "You annoy him, but half of that is because he's attracted to you."

A flash of heat rushes through me at the thought.

There is something seriously wrong with me.

I just cannot understand why I'm so attracted to that jerk. So what if he's hotter than Hades? He's arrogant and pushy and demanding and so full of himself.

Lia giggles.

"What?"

"You're blushing." Max grins. "The sparks really fly when the two of you are together. I say go for it."

"Max! Don't encourage that."

I'd been about to deny everything, but Lia's horror annoys me.

"Why not?" Max asks what I'm thinking.

"If she and Finn get together, Ainsley will target her something fierce."

"I haven't even spoken one word to this Ainsley person," I protest. "I think you must be exaggerating."

"I'm not," Lia insists.

"Yeah, I hate to say it, but she's right," Max says.

"Well, I'm not worried about it," I say. "I doubt there's a single person in this school who could take me, including all of the professors and Finn himself."

Max grins. "I'm sure you're right. And honestly, with the amount of heat you two give off, I imagine it'd probably be worth it."

I raise an eyebrow. "So, what about you, Max? You attracted to Finn? Or are you more into girls? Or both?"

He shrugs. "Mainly girls. I haven't met a guy yet who's made me change my mind on that, but you never know."

I grin. "I like it. Nice and flexible. How about you, Lia?"

She blushes. "Boys all the way."

I nod. "Okay. So here's the next question. Max, imagine a world where you and Brittany give off sparks something fierce. Would it be worth it?"

He makes a face. "Not even for all the chocolate in the world."

Chapter Eight

BY THE END of the first week, we've fallen into a pattern that repeats itself as the semester slowly marches forward.

Each morning, I meet Max and Lia in the cafeteria for breakfast.

Finn usually joins us at some point and immediately starts arguing with me about something he's clearly been stewing over.

Over the weeks, we've reached a sort of detente where we're able to hash out our differences and come to some semblance of a compromise in our assignments.

It's a constant battle, though, partly because we're both so stubborn, and partly, honestly, because I'm a Criminal and we take perverse pleasure in riling people up.

The more we argue and debate, struggle for compromise and frankly, threaten each other with dismemberment, the hotter the attraction burns.

When he gets all riled up, a lock of his hair falls into his eyes and he shoves it back with this impatient gesture and then ends up waving his arms and pacing back and forth while ranting, and frankly, I can't help but watch and melt a little inside.

He's just too beautiful for words.

After two and a half months of these constant interactions with him, I've pretty much come to terms with the fact that I find him dead sexy and will probably never get over it.

Instead, I've learned to live with it.

Obviously, I'm damaged in some way, but there you have it.

The truth is I rile him up just so that I can sit back and enjoy his ranting, partly because he's so good at it—he's got quite the way with words—but mostly because he's poetry in motion.

And so the days and nights go by, with both of us ignoring the attraction that burns ever brighter.

Clearly, he's learned to live with it too.

Which is why it's such a shock one evening when Finn just stops in the middle of a rant, sets his hands on his hips and stares at the floor while breathing deeply.

It's not that he stopped, it's that he stopped so soon.

I'm eyeing his many attributes, wondering if I can rile him up again, just so that I can watch him shove back that lock of hair once more, when he whirls and lunges.

I'm so taken by surprise, I don't even try to defend myself.

And then I don't want to.

One minute, I'm sitting in my chair, lusting after the arrogant jerk, the next I'm in his arms and he's kissing me.

And oh, what a kiss!

We break apart and stare at one another, then lunge back together and kiss some more.

"This isn't good," I mutter, even as I try to get closer.

"Not at all," he agrees.

A loud bang reverberates through the library and we jerk apart, breathing heavily.

"Right," he says. "I think we'd better call it a night."

"I agree. We're on for this weekend, right?"

"Of course. We've been planning for weeks now. Time to set things in motion."

I nod. "All right then. I'll see you tomorrow in class."

"Right." He gathers up his books and walks away.

He doesn't look back.

I collapse into my chair and work on catching my breath.

What in all of Faerie just happened and why does it feel as if we've unleashed the inevitable?

The next day, Lia, Max and I are heading to the cafeteria for lunch when Aisling, Brittany and several of their friends shove their way into our path.

We're in the main lobby, not far from our destination, but just far enough from the classrooms and the cafeteria, for them to obviously feel safe in confronting us.

There are no professors nearby.

"What's up, Aisling?" I ask. "Brittany." I nod to them both.

"What's up is you thinking you can come into this school and take whatever you want."

I raise an eyebrow. "No idea what you're talking about, Aisling."

"Liar. Finn's mine and you're going to stay away from him."

Ah. Should have known. I bet she had a spy in the library with us and that was probably the bang we heard: someone rushing out the door to give her their report.

Awesome.

"I'm warning you. Stay away from Finn or I will end you." Aisling whirls around and storms off, her posse surrounding her.

I roll my eyes. I may not be interested in pursuing this weird attraction with Finn (okay, yes, I am, but I'm never admitting it to anyone), but I'm also not about to let this entitled stalker push me around.

"I'm sorry," I say loudly to her back. "Was that supposed to be a threat? Because I'm really not feeling it."

You could hear a pin drop in the silence that follows.

Aisling turns and storms back toward me, fury written all over her. "You have no idea who you're dealing with if you think—"

"Actually, Aisling, *you're* the one without a clue and this is the only warning I'm going to give you: you don't want to get on my bad side. You have no idea what I'm capable of."

"You think I'm scared of some lowlife Criminal?" Ainsley demands.

I grin. "I'm guessing no, but then it's clear you're just not that smart."

Ainsley gasps, then swings out in fury.

Of course, I'm ready for that response. She telegraphs her moves long before she makes them, probably because she allows her anger to take control.

I sketch a symbol in the air.

It's one I learned at age seven when I was almost kidnapped by one of my aunt's enemies. The entire extended family got involved, teaching me and the twins and our cousins every defensive and offensive spell they felt we were capable of learning at the time. From that moment forward, we were trained day in and day out, with only one goal in mind: safety.

These children had no idea who now walked in their midst.

Everyone in the hall was frozen. Ainsley was hanging mid-air, in the middle of her uncontrolled lunge at me.

Her eyes pinwheeled in her face, but otherwise, she was unable to move.

"You do understand that I've been training since I was a babe to wreak havoc upon society, right?" I slowly circle her figure, trailing one finger down her side, then back up the other.

Outside our little bubble, time had slowed to a fraction of its normal speed.

I stop in front of Ainsley and stare into her terrified eyes. I lean forward to whisper in her ear, "If I wanted, I could slit your throat right now."

I step back and allow her to see the beast that lies dormant inside.

It's a bloodthirsty thing, that wild Fae Criminal who lives to wreak not just havoc, not just chaos, but utter destruction in all its forms.

I keep a firm leash on the wildness at all times, just like all Criminals do, but sometimes I allow that leash to slip just a little. Mostly in times like this, when I feel for their own safety, I must allow others to see the beast peeking out from my eyes and to know how close to death they've truly come.

"So here's the deal, Ainsley. You avoid me. Don't look at me. Don't speak to me. And I'll do you the favor of not taking you out. Or even better of ruining your life." In a move so fast, I doubt she even saw it, I pull my knife from my belt and slice a three inch lock from her dark hair. "Next time, if I'm feeling generous, maybe I'll just shave your head and carve up your pretty little face."

I sheathe my knife again, take one sliding step to the side and snap my fingers.

The bubble pops, time unfreezes and Ainsley sails through the air, her lunge now in freefall.

She slams to the ground with a groan.

I stare down at her. "Don't test me, Ainsley. You won't like the results."

I drop her lock of hair so that it falls to the floor right in front of her eyes, then walk past her, through the silent crowds and into the cafeteria.

I get my food and settle at the Year One table, and am honestly shocked when Max and Lia join me moments later.

"That was awesome," Lia says.

"I wish I'd had my mirror ready," Max says. "I would have given anything to get a recording of that."

A tiny part of me that was already mourning the loss of their friendship relaxes in relief.

I smile back at them. "You don't think I went too far?"

Max and Lia hadn't been caught in either Ainsley's bubble or in the time warp.

I'd deliberately allowed them to stay with me in real time, partly because they're my friends and I wouldn't feel right casting a spell upon them, and partly because I felt they deserved to know who it is they've actually befriended.

"Of course not," Lia says.

"It was genius of you to threaten to shave her," Max says. "She's so certain of her own power and abilities, she might have blown off a threat to kill her, but she'll never risk waking up bald."

Lia snickers. "I'd give anything to see it happen though."

The rest of the day is fairly uneventful, mainly because Finn is acting incredibly weird.

He doesn't argue with me once in either of our final two classes of the day, but instead just stares at me as if he's never seen me before.

I'd think it's a reaction to our unexpected make-out session the night before, but he acted perfectly normal during our morning classes, so I'm guessing he's heard about the confrontation with Ainsley.

Except Max and Lia wouldn't have told him anything, and everyone else was caught in the time warp so would have seen very little.

Basically, they'd have seen Ainsley lunging toward me and then when time sped up again, they would have seen me in a different place from where I'd started and Ainsley on the floor with a tiny lock of her hair.

It's probably the hair that did it.

I enjoyed that demonstration of my power and Max thought it was brilliant, but it also was something that couldn't easily be explained, which is probably why Finn's staring at me so strangely.

Just when I'm certain he's not going to mention it, he finally says, "I heard you took out Ainsley."

I shrug. "Pretty sure she took herself out."

"Yeah, if you think I believe that, you're insane. Ainsley and I grew up in the same town and went to the same pre-academy schools. She's beaten down more girls over the years than I can count. You're the first to walk away from a confrontation without a single scratch.

"Actually, you're the first to walk away at all. Most are unconscious after Ainsley targets them. Then they either join her crew or avoid her like the plague."

I roll my eyes. "Yeah, neither of those options work for me."

He lets out a soft snort. "Clearly not."

A few moments later, the bell rings, signaling the end of classes for the day and Finn asks, "Are we meeting to study after dinner?"

I shrug. "If you want to. Can't hurt to go over the plan one final time."

We're scheduled to spend the weekend in Midnight Falls, along with Max and Lia, spying on our targets and setting them up.

For what is still up for debate. All I'm really sure of is that it's *not* True Love.

"Sounds good," Finn says. "See you tonight."

"Yeah, later."

At dinner that evening, I try to recruit Max and Lia to join us in the library, but they're onto me.

"Something set off Ainsley and I'm guessing it had to do with you and Finn in the library last night," Max says.

"What makes you say that?"

Lia giggles.

"What?"

"You're blushing again," Max says.

How annoying. "I'm fairly certain Criminals aren't allowed to blush."

Max lets out a snort. "Maybe that's why you're a Godparent and not a Criminal."

"I beg to differ. I'm pretty sure I'm a Criminal Godparent or some such thing."

Lia giggles. "That'd be pretty cool actually. Don't you think?"

I roll my eyes. "Only if you mean cool in the sense that my only other option is to just be a Godparent. Because in that case, yes, adding Criminal to the mix provides a much-needed element of cool."

Before they can reply, Finn shows up. "You ready?"

"Aren't you going to eat?"

"I've got a plate for later."

I shrug. "All right then. You guys sure you don't want to join us?"

"Nah, we're good," Lia says.

Five minutes later, Finn and I are settled at a table in the library, going over the plan.

"So we're just going to pop in and get a sense for all the players tomorrow, right?" Finn asks.

"Exactly. We'll then spend tomorrow night debriefing and making a plan for Sunday."

We've spent the last couple months observing what we can through our mirrors, but I've continually complained that they just don't show everything and we're hampered without an in-person analysis of each of our targets' personalities and circumstances.

"Are we certain we want to start at the manor and not the palace?"

I want to scream that we've already gone over this a million times, but I did agree to meet with him to go over the plan, even though we both know it backward and forward, so I can't really complain if he's doing just that.

Still, I'm sick of this conversation and my dragonmark is itching something fierce, which just makes me crankier.

I drag in a deep breath and repeat an old argument for the

hundredth time. "The palace is huge. It's going to take a while for us to track down each of the Charmings. We need to get the smaller place out of the way first. The manor, *then* the palace."

We talk in circles for another thirty minutes before Finn is finally satisfied.

We pack up our books and walk back to the Aphrodite Wing together. We part in the area between the doors to our towers and promise to meet back where we're standing at dawn.

He looks like he wants to kiss me goodnight, but there are entirely too many students still up, studying and talking in the common area, all of them clearly interested in what we're up to.

"See you tomorrow, Finn," I say.

"Yeah. Tomorrow, Mari."

Chapter Nine

I MEET UP with Lia right outside my room and we walk down to the common room together where we find Max and Finn waiting.

Or rather, Max is waiting a bit off to the side, arms crossed, scowl on his face as he watches Aisling and Brittany cozy up to Finn, who just looks uncomfortable.

The girls are standing on either side of him. Aisling has one hand on his arm and is looking up at him with an earnest expression on her face.

Brittany is just nodding her head in agreement at whatever it is Aisling is saying.

"What do you want to bet they're trying to invite themselves along?" I mutter to Lia.

She gives me a horrified look. "They can't possibly, right? I mean they'd need a weekend pass and we got ours more than a month ago."

"I doubt they worry about anything so banal as the rules."

Lia grimaces. "Let's go rescue Max."

We walk across the common room toward them.

Max's face lights up when he sees us and he hurries toward us.

Surprisingly, Finn's face lights up as well.

He shakes off Aisling's hand and follows Max to meet us in the center of the room. "Ready?" His eyes are on me when he asks the question.

I nod.

"Awesome. I've already picked up our breakfast. I figure we can eat on the way."

We make our way through the castle, across the courtyard and into the stables where our horses have been prepped and are waiting for us.

I greet Bladerunner with a kiss to his nose and a stroke of his head before walking him out into the sunlight and mounting him.

We set out at a slow lope, circling around the castle toward the back where a second drawbridge waits.

We show our weekend passes to the guardsman, who lowers the bridge, and we ride across in a thunder of hooves.

The castle sits on land heavy with the magic of Faerie and is dead center in the middle of a series of faerie rings that stretch outward for miles. We're headed for the fifth ring, to one small spot where all the lines of all the realms converge.

It's about a two hour ride from the castle and Finn provides us each with a hunk of faerie bread to munch along the way.

Once we're far enough away from the castle, Max and Lia, who are riding ahead of Finn and me, give each other a grin, then let out a loud whoop and take off, riding across the land at a thunderous pace.

It's tempting to chase after them, but I restrain myself. I'm more interested in quizzing Finn.

"So what did those two want this morning?" I peek up at him through my lashes.

He's staring straight ahead, an unreadable expression on his face. "Just to talk about an assignment."

"Their matches?"

"Yeah."

"Are theirs in Midnight Falls too?"

"No. They're in Kings Valley."

Well, that's a relief. No chance of running into those two this weekend. "Are they going there?"

"No. They were pretty much horrified at the thought of it. They think we're crazy for wanting to interact with our matches."

"Yeah, well, I think it's crazy it's not standard practice."

"Well, I guess we'll find out soon enough whether it's a good idea or not."

We talk for a while longer before agreeing to pick up the pace.

"Race you to the creek in the third ring," Finn says.

"You're on!" I lean over and whisper in Bladerunner's ear "Let's ride like the wind, my love."

As if he's been waiting for just those words, Bladerunner lunges forward and we're off.

The ride is utterly exhilarating, with the wind racing through my hair, the land barreling by, the feel of Bladerunner beneath me, his power unleashed, and Finn and his mount Larkspur racing to my left.

We reach the creek to find Max and Lia waiting for us there. We dismount and walk the horses to the water. While they're drinking, we take a short break to enjoy the freedom and the quiet.

Soon enough, though, we're up and riding again.

There's a small gatekeeper's cottage right in the middle of the fifth ring and that's where we're headed.

The gatekeeper is waiting for us.

He's an older Fae, with a shock of white hair, a grouchy disposition and a stern demeanor.

It takes millennia for a Fae's hair to turn white—that is if the Fae isn't born that way—so he must be very old indeed.

"It's about time," he growls at us. "The day's half done already."

Since we left the castle just as the sun was rising over the hills, I seriously doubt that, but I just nod respectfully, as do the others.

"Sorry we're late," Finn says. "We stopped the horses for a bit of a drink halfway here."

"Should have calculated the break into your schedule. Left fifteen minutes early, but too late for that now. You'll know for next time."

He begins to pace in front of us. "Now here are the rules. No funny business. No changing fates. No magic for the sake of magic. Any spells are to be for the specific purpose of achieving a match. Also. No falling in love."

I startle. "Excuse me?"

"You're going into Midnight Falls to match others, *not* to match yourselves."

"Is that really a danger?" I ask, honestly curious about it.

"It's been known to happen, but rarely. Not so much anymore since the old ways have died out. Good for you for taking the time to reenact this tradition."

"Tradition?" Lia asks tentatively.

"Interacting with the matches is a time-honored tradition, one that's fallen to the wayside with the younger generations. Lazy, that's the problem these days! Well, come along then."

He leads us through the cottage to an enclosed courtyard at the back.

In the center of the courtyard, we can see the ripple in space where the lines all converge.

"Give me a moment to find the right line." He strides toward the ripples and begins to pluck lines apart, slowly unraveling and separating them until he extracts one small fold in space.

He spreads his hands and the fold widens.

He pinches a tiny corner of it, then flicks it away and the fold widens again, expanding into a doorway.

On the other side is another courtyard that looks remarkably like the one we're standing in.

"Well, go on then, I haven't got all day."

"Thank you, Keeper." I bow my head to him before passing through the Veil.

We're met on the other side by yet another Gatekeeper. This one is a female with dark black hair and piercing blue eyes.

"Welcome to Midnight Falls. Follow me." She turns and leads the way into the rest of the house we're now standing in.

It's much bigger than the gatehouse we left in Faerie.

She leads us to a reception desk, where she plucks two keys off a wall and hands one over to me and one to Finn. She spins a book around to face us. "Sign in."

We each sign our names, then she leads us up a flight of stairs and down a short hall. She stops at the end of the hall between two doors that are directly across from each other. "Boys are here on the right.

Girls on the left. Breakfast is at six sharp. Lunch is at noon. Dinner is at six. If you're late, you don't eat. You're to be checked out and on your way no later than seven tomorrow evening. I don't advise waiting that late though unless you want to be riding home in the dark. Good luck with your mission. Remember: magic is only to be used in this realm to accomplish your matches." She turns to walk away.

"Right then. Why don't you two drop off your things, then meet us in our room," Finn says.

Three minutes later, we're all in Finn and Max's room and we have a game plan. We agree we'll have lunch while out, but will meet back here for dinner at six.

Max and Lia's targets are all close by, in the town we're now staying in, so they leave the house by the front door, intending to walk toward their targets.

Our targets, on the other hand, are a bit further away so we cast a couple simple spells—one a bit of glamour to hide us from mortal eyes and a second to mute our voices behind a bubble so we can discuss what we see without being heard.

We then mirror-walk to our destination.

We arrive inside the Brighton manor, where Cinderella lives with her stepmother and two stepsisters, and discover chaos.

The stepmother, Margaret, is an absolute nightmare, barking out orders to Cinderella, who is dressed literally in rags and is running back and forth to meet the many demands Margaret throws at her.

The stepsisters are barely a step down from the nightmare of their mother, still demanding and rude, but not quite so harsh.

"I'm beginning to understand why she has no last name," I mutter to Finn. "Who would want to share a name with those three?"

He lets out a snort. "I think it has more to do with the fact that they're not really related."

"Yes, but what about her father? Surely she was given his name or her mother's."

He shrugs. "Who knows? Perhaps it was forgotten over the years."

"Hurry up, Cinderella. I don't have all day, you know!" The demand sounds much worse coming from the older stepsister, Bethany, than it did from the elderly gatekeeper.

"She needs to get my slippers first," the younger sister, Harriet exclaims.

"You can wait until after she's brought me my breakfast," Bethany says.

"Here." Cinderella hurries into the room, a tray balanced on one hand and a pair of slippers in the other. She drops the slippers to the floor in front of Harriet, then delivers plates from the tray to each of the three women seated at the table.

"These eggs are cold," Margaret says, her voice arctic.

"Mine are runny," Bethany whines.

"They're sunny side up," I mutter to Finn. "Aren't they supposed to be runny?"

He lets out a snort of laughter.

"Cinderella, what on earth are you wearing?" Harriet sneers.

Cinderella pauses and looks down at her—I'm not even sure what to call it. It's literally a piece of fabric that's in tatters hanging from her shoulders. Maybe at one time it was a dress, but now it's pretty much unidentifiable. "It's the only thing I have," she says.

Finn inhales sharply.

I know exactly what he's thinking because I'm thinking it too.

"These girls are unbelievable. How are we supposed to match *them*?"

"Yeah, well, I think our bigger problem's going to be Cinderella and just getting her out of the house to meet her match," Finn says.

Yeah, that's a problem, all right.

Cinderella's been identified as the match for the oldest Prince Charming—Adam.

Finn thinks it's because they're a perfect match.

I, however, do not agree.

After all, this isn't the first time we've spied on Cinderella and her sisters or on the princes Charming, though this is the first time we've done it in person. All the other times have been via the mirror.

The problem with spying through a mirror is the limited view the mirror provides, not to mention the limited amount of time. At most, you can observe for about two or three minutes before the picture goes fuzzy and the sound disappears.

What this means is that until this very moment, we've only had tiny glimpses of what life is like for Cinderella and the Brighton sisters.

Observing them in person has really blown the entire thing wide open.

I'm realizing exactly how difficult these matches will be to accomplish, and I can tell by the look on Finn's face that he agrees.

I rub my dragonmark, taking comfort in the feel of the dragon's scales against my skin.

This is so discouraging.

"At least all we have to do with Cinderella is get her into the presence of the prince," Finn says. "Once they're together, the power of True Love should work its magic."

All I have to say to that is ugh.

Okay, no, I have more to say about it.

I know Finn's convinced the matches identified by the powers-that-be are flawless in every way, but there's no way this particular match is anything but a disaster in the making.

The few glimpses we've had of Adam Charming through the mirror have made that perfectly clear.

Let's just say that he should have been named Prince Not–So–Charming instead. In fact, after observing Bethany and Harriet, I'd say he's a better match for one of them than for poor Cinderella.

"Mother," Harriet screeches. "We've been invited to the Palace for the royal ball."

"Let me see that." Bethany grabs for the invitation and the two of them engage in a tug-of-war until their mother reaches between them and snatches the card right out of their hands.

"Read it, Mother," Bethany begs.

"The King and Queen of Midnight Falls invite all eligible citizens to attend this year's Royal Ball, to be presented to the Princess and the Princes Charming for their hands in marriage."

Bethany and Harriet let out identical squeals of joy and excitement.

"A ball," Cinderella says in amazement. "And we're *all* invited to attend."

The other women freeze, then turn and stare at Cinderella.

"You?" Margaret exclaims. "You cannot possibly go to the ball. You have nothing to wear and if you think I'm going to spend any money on you, well, forget that. Besides, it would be a complete waste. As if you would ever catch the eye of a prince." She turns to her daughters. "We have no time to lose, ladies. We'll need to make arrangements for the dressmaker and the hairdresser and oh my goodness, I can see it now. Each of my daughters married to a prince. Eventually, I'll be the mother of a queen, the grandmother of kings."

I roll my eyes. This woman is too much.

Finn nudges me and nods toward Cinderella.

She's standing, hands clenched, a mutinous look on her face, glaring at her stepmother.

"I'm not interested in catching the eye of any prince," Cinderella snaps.

All three women turn back to stare at her in surprise.

"Are you stupid?" Bethany demands.

"She doesn't even realize the opportunity we've been afforded," Harriet says.

Margaret just laughs. "So what *are* you interested in then? Playing in cinders, cleaning fireplaces, your entire life?"

"It's better than hooking my stars to the delusion of True Love," Cinderella says.

"True love?" Bethany and Harriet chorus, then burst into laughter.

"Who cares about True Love if the man you're marrying is rich and powerful?" Margaret demands.

"Well, as it happens, I don't care to get married at all," Cinderella says, "not for love, not for money, not even for power."

A girl after my own heart.

"Then you really *are* stupid," Bethany says.

"Marriage is just a disaster waiting to happen," Cinderella says, "and True Love is even worse."

She's speaking my language now.

"I mean, look at your life, Stepmother."

Margaret freezes and spears Cinderella with an icy cold glare.

"What is that supposed to mean?"

"Married for True Love to their father, didn't you? And when he died, he left you without a penny and heartbroken to boot. Forced to marry lower than your perceived station in life, forced to live here, in this rundown manor, forced to care for the stepdaughter you hate, and all for what? For True Love in the first case and for money in the second. Not a lot of money, to be sure, but more than you had. And in both cases, *still* left alone to struggle on your own. Might as well have tried from the very beginning to be strong and capable and support yourself, rather than hitch your fortunes to the backs of men who would ultimately let you down by dying on you."

Silence falls in the wake of Cinderella's diatribe.

Margaret had paled to sheet white and her daughters didn't look much better.

"Get out of here," Margaret hisses, a stricken look on her face.

"You know I'm right." Cinderella glares back at her. "And no matter what you think, Margaret, I am sorry for it. Sorry you've lost so much in your life, but even sorrier those losses have rotted you through to the core and taken your daughters with you."

She turns away from Margaret and walks across the room toward the stairs that lead to the attic. "Besides," she mutters as she sweeps by us, "if I were going to try and hook a royal, I'd go for the *Princess* Charming rather than her testosterone-ridden brothers."

My eyes widen and I let out a snort of laughter at the look on Finn's face. There go all his delusions of a True Love match between Cinderella and Adam Charming.

Movement from across the room catches my eye.

Margaret reaches out a hand, grabs the back of a chair and slowly sinks into it, the look of sorrow and grief on her face ending my hilarity.

Cinderella's words have clearly found their mark.

"Mother, are you okay?" Harriet asks tentatively.

"Just leave me, girls."

"But the dressmaker. If we don't reach out now, we'll never get an appointment," Bethany says.

Margaret sighs. "Fine. Bring me my mirror."

Chapter Ten

FINN IS SO annoyed when we leave the manor, he insists we walk to the palace, which is frankly impossible in the time we have, but I can tell he needs to walk off his mad, so I agree.

And for the next I don't even know how long, I get to listen to him rant.

"This is supposed to be a love match. If Cinderella's attracted to women, I don't see how we're going to get her to fall in love with the prince."

"I think it's pretty obvious we're not going to manage that," I say, "so it's time to pivot."

"Pivot? What's that supposed to mean? Pivot?"

"The ball's in three weeks. That gives us plenty of time to figure out how we're going to get Cinderella to the ball and introduce her to Princess Adriana."

"Are you serious right now?"

"Absolutely."

"But Adriana's not in line for the throne," Finn protests.

"I don't see why not. According to our paperwork, she's the oldest. I'm pretty sure that's how it works. The oldest inherits the throne."

"Unless they're female," Finn says.

"That can't be right."

"Afraid it is. Humans are a little weird about gender."

"But there have been plenty of female monarchs throughout human history."

"Sure. When there wasn't a male to inherit the throne."

"No way." I think about it a minute and realize he's right. At least for this particular kingdom and quite a few others I can think of off the top of my head. "Okay, so we just need to get this antiquated, completely misogynistic law changed."

"Don't be ridiculous. We can't interfere with human laws."

"But this is what the Fae want, right? The papers on Cinderella made it clear they want her positioned as co-ruler of the Midnight Falls Kingdom. This is the perfect solution."

"We can't go around messing with human laws and politics. We're in the business of making True Love matches, not political ones."

"Finn, I hate to say this, but if you truly believe that, you're delusional. What do you think just happened in there? The powers-that-be told us to match Cinderella with the heir to the throne. The heir is male. Cinderella's into females. This does not compute. The only way it makes sense is if the Fae are trying to arrange a political match, not a True Love one."

Finn sighs. "Even if that's true, I have no idea how to go about getting laws changed, especially human ones. That just feels like an impossible task."

I groan. Well, if he doesn't like that suggestion, I can pretty much guarantee he's not going to like my next one. "So just for clarification. If there are no male heirs, a female can inherit the throne?"

"Exactly."

"So there's your solution. We'll get the FCA involved."

Finn stares at me in horror. "The Fae Criminal Agency? Are you crazy? They're a bunch of assassins and psychos. I don't think they're going to want to work on changing any laws."

"First of all, some of my relatives work for the FCA, thank you very much, and secondly, that's *not* what we'd be calling them in for."

"Unbelievable." Finn shook his head. "You're seriously suggesting we recruit the FCA to take out the princes."

I shrug. "If the Fae want Cinderella on the throne of Midnight Falls, it may become necessary."

Finn stares at me like he's never seen me before.

I let out a huff of exasperation. "Look, I'm not saying it's right. I'm just saying the Fae can't always manipulate everyone and every situation. People have free will and trying to get someone who likes one gender to marry an entirely different gender sounds pretty impossible to me.

"It'd be easier to get her to marry the gender she's attracted to and then deal with any barriers to the throne after that."

"So, we match Cinderella with Princess Adriana and then we somehow manipulate the situation so Adriana inherits the throne instead of Prince Adam?"

"Exactly. Should be easy enough. Though I'd like to point out this entire conversation has pretty much proven my point. What we're talking about has nothing to do with arranging a True Love match. Instead, we're focused on Cinderella marrying the throne by the most expedient way possible. In other words, we're indulging in political machinations."

Finn groaned. "Fine. You win. They're not love matches at this point. Although let's be clear, *you're* the one who brought up the possibility of having three of our targets assassinated rather than matched with their True Loves, something that is clearly beyond the parameters of our assignment."

"True. And now that I think about it, that could be a tiny barrier to us passing this course." I pause a moment, then add cheerfully, "But I'm sure we can come up with a better plan. Eventually."

"Let's just get to the palace and track down the Charmings and the Brighton brother. We'll get a feel for their personalities and hopefully, an idea of the kind of person who would be a good match for them. Maybe we'll get lucky and we can match one of them with Bethany or Harriet."

"Ugh. I wouldn't match a flea with either one of them. This is a terrible assignment. You know that, right?"

"Eh, it's not so bad. Beautiful weather, change of scenery, good company." He winks at me.

I roll my eyes. "Whatever. Can we stop walking now and use a mirror to get where we're going, please?"

The palace is *still* far in the distance, even though we've been walking for almost an hour now.

"Fine." He pulls out his mirror and opens the paperwork with the images of our targets. "Shall we start with the heir himself?"

"Works for me."

He taps Adam's picture and it fades to a room in the palace, where it appears Adam is eating and berating a servant.

Finn reaches into the mirror, pinches a tiny fold in space and pulls the scene toward us, or at least that's how it feels. In reality we're folded into the scene and a second later, find ourselves swaying in one of the dining halls of the palace.

I'm almost immediately left with a feeling of deja vu as the crown prince dresses down pretty much everyone in his vicinity. It feels very much like a repeat of what we observed in the manor with the Brighton women. This scene just has different players.

"Great," I say to Finn. "So let me recap." I tick off our targets on my fingers.

"We have Cinderella, who is rebellious, anti-marriage, anti-True Love and completely into girls.

"We have Bethany and Harriet, who are total witches in disguise, unattractive and hateful in the extreme.

"And now we have the crown prince, Adam, an arrogant, pompous ass."

"That pretty much sums it up," Finn says glumly.

"Well, I have two predictions based on this new information."

"All right, let's hear them."

"One, our assignment is doomed—"

"Don't say that!"

"—and two, this kingdom is doomed as well."

"Great."

"Personally I would say either Bethany or Harriet would be the perfect match for this particular Prince Charming. The only problem is —"

"That would mean one of those two horrid women would end up in charge of an entire kingdom?"

"Exactly. Bad enough he's in charge. Are we sure he's the heir?"

"Unfortunately, yes."

We spend the rest of the day trying to track down the other three Charmings, but we're always a step behind one of them.

We finally retire to the cottage where we're staying and spend the evening with Lia and Max, comparing notes.

They had a lot more progress than we did. They found all of their matches and have figured out who most of them should be with.

They're already deep into the planning phase of how to get their targets and intended matches together to see if the spark of True Love is ignited.

I have to roll my eyes at this description, but otherwise, I'm a little envious of the ease of their assignments compared to ours.

We hang out in the boys' room for hours after dinner, strategizing and talking.

Finn and I have no solutions and feel that we can't really begin to fully strategize a plan until we have a good grasp on who all the players are.

After our observations of half our targets, Finn has conceded that in-person observations are critical to the success of a True Love mission and he's now questioning whether that mission is just a front for political machinations.

I can't help but grin.

Seriously.

I did that.

If I hadn't asked the questions and kept pushing for this, Finn,

Max and Lia would all still believe the lie.

And I do think it's a lie.

The real question circles around how deep the lie actually goes.

Has it infiltrated every single match or are most matches True Love matches, thus giving the mission credibility and obscuring the truth so that one or two or ten political matches can slide through unnoticed?

The next day Finn and I are back at the palace, tracking down our targets. We catch all of the Charmings at breakfast and have an opportunity to observe them in action.

It's obvious to me, barely five minutes in, that of the four siblings, Adriana is the one who should inherit the throne.

In the absence of their parents, who are apparently away for the weekend, she presides over the breakfast table with grace and nobility and clearly has a strong relationship with each one of her brothers.

She draws the youngest brother, Lyle, who is epically shy, even among family, out of his shell and gets him talking about his plans for the day. He lights up as he describes his art.

She encourages the middle brother, Victor, to stay true to himself, to go after what he wants and to not worry about what anyone else thinks. There seems to be some subtext there I'm not getting, but it's clear her words are meaningful and precious to Victor.

As for the heir, Adam, she seems to bring out the best in him. When he seems about to snap at one of the maids, Adriana places her hand over his on the table and squeezes it lightly. Without a word, she changes his entire demeanor. He murmurs a thank you to the maid instead of berating her and is on his best behavior for the rest of the meal.

"Okay," Finn says, "you're right. We'll focus on getting Cinderella to the ball and then on getting her and Adriana together. Whether or not Adriana takes the throne, I'm convinced they would make a good match."

We spend the rest of the day following the various siblings around the palace. We also manage to track down Bethany and Harriet's older brother, Lord Brighton, who turns out to be Victor's best friend.

Within minutes of observing the dynamics between Lord Brighton and Prince Victor, I'm convinced we have at least one match that will be easily made.

I nudge Finn, who is busy tapping away at his mirror, rather than paying attention to the mission, and when I have his attention, nod toward Victor and Steven.

The two are leaning over a map, discussing some construction work that's being done at the palace, but the body language is saying more than their words.

"Well, hallelujah," Finn mutters. "Finally, an easy match. Now all we have to do is get them to kiss."

"Really?" I roll my eyes. "That's all it takes? Just one kiss?"

"If it's True Love's kiss, absolutely. Well, most of the time."

I groan. "And when might it not work?"

"Well, if one of them is a little resistant to the idea of True Love, they may not actually recognize the kiss when it happens."

I groan. "So basically a kiss between Cinderella and Adriana isn't going to cut it."

He shrugs. "Depends on how much of what Cinderella was saying about not believing or wanting True Love was truth. Sometimes we say what we think is our truth, but there's something else buried deep. If we're lucky, Cinderella still harbors a tiny bit of hope. Even the smallest spark can set off a blaze.”

“So how do we get these two to kiss?”

He glances down at his mirror. “Well, it’s not going to happen today. We’re due at the cottage in about five minutes.”

“Fine. At least we have three more weeks to figure out our strategy. I think the ball is where it’s all going to happen.”

“Even for the Brighton sisters?”

I grimace. “Well, maybe not for them. Or for Prince Not-So-Charming Adam. But otherwise, I have a good feeling about these two and about Cinderella and Adriana.”

Finn grins. “Glad to hear it. Now let’s go home.”

Chapter Eleven

THE FOLLOWING THREE weeks are intensely busy as we head toward finals.

Between classes and long hours studying with Finn (and by studying, I mean making out), I'm not getting a whole lot of sleep.

On a side note, though, I'm being thoroughly entertained by the multiple attempts to break into my room.

I think it's become a bit of a dare among the upper levels to see if they can outwit the Criminal.

They can't, of course, but nevertheless, they keep trying.

One weekend, there are no less than seven individuals walking around the Academy with the word "THIEF" branded across their foreheads.

I did mention the punishment spells embedded in the lock mechanisms, right?

I honestly can't understand why the students keep trying. I've never seen such persistence when confronted with the aftereffects of an attempt to break into a space claimed by a Criminal. Perhaps the pressure from all the studying has gotten to them.

I keep expecting some form of retaliation, but bizarrely, no one seems upset at their ongoing failures. In fact, the students seem to find the entire exercise hilarious and seem to be egging each other on.

Even stranger than that, upper level students have begun approaching me in the hallways and at meals to ask if I'd like to study with them or to hang out.

Finn finds this to be extremely annoying and has threatened violence no less than nineteen times in the last forty-eight hours.

Max and Lia, on the other hand, find it all supremely entertaining and hilarious.

As for me, I'm just annoyed at all the attention.

I'm used to flying under the radar, for Fae's sake.

One good thing has resulted from the increase in my reputation though.

Aisling and Brittany have not only left me alone since my little demonstration of power last month, but they're also actively avoiding Finn, Max and Lia.

I'd feel bad about it, but since I don't really like either one of them, I'm celebrating instead.

Well, celebrating and studying (and by studying, I still mean making out) and obsessing over the state of our matches with Finn.

The final exam for Matchmaking 101 is to write a report on the progress we've made toward achieving Love Matches for our targets.

As we've made zero progress so far and everything depends on a ball we're not even sure we can get all of our targets to attend, Finn and

I have been a little testy with each other lately.

That testiness usually results in an intense make-out session that leaves me craving more.

At this point, I've pretty much moved beyond being resigned that I find Finn attractive as hell to the next stage of our relationship's development, which is being resigned to the fact that we have one.

I know.

He's still a jerk, but then I'm still a Criminal, so I guess that's fine then.

I mean, it isn't really fair to expect someone to change who they are, is it?

I still have no idea why I ended up here at the FGA rather than at the HCA, but I've decided I don't care because I love it here.

Bizarre, right?

Of course, I still think the whole True Love thing is nothing but a hoax, possibly a mass hallucination, and definitely an attempt by the Throne to expand its reach and control.

So that part's not really any better.

However, I love Max and Lia and I definitely enjoy my time with Finn.

I miss the twins and my cousins, of course, and it was hard seeing them over fall break because we're already growing apart.

We have entire lives we're leading separate from each other, lives that are full of stories and new friendships and paths that are leading us further and further away from each other.

I would feel that loss so much more deeply were it not for Max and Lia. They keep me sane, as does Finn, though I really hate to admit it.

In addition, much to my surprise, I'm truly enjoying my classes. I've become something of an expert at derailing our lessons to ask questions or to make pointed observations that our teachers often struggle to answer or dispute in any logical way.

Like when Finn and I provide a very detailed report of what we discovered about Cinderella and her Fae-sanctioned, doomed match with Adam Charming in our Matchmaking 101 class.

The students had a ton of questions and afterward, Professor Halloran was inundated with requests to observe targets in person.

I think it's an excellent development.

I'm not sure the teachers agree, but since no one has told me to stop talking in class, I guess they don't mind too much.

The only worry I have at this point is that we may not pass our classes if we can't get our matches moving forward. We do have a plan, though, and by plan, I mean a to-do list. It looks something like this:

1. Get Cinderella to the ball.
2. Get Cinderella and Princess Adriana to dance.
3. Get Prince Victor and Lord Brighton to kiss.
4. Observe Prince Adam and Prince Lyle and identify potential matches for each of them.*
5. Observe Bethany and Harriet and identify potential matches for each of them.*

***Note:** *under no circumstances should any of the individuals in step 4 be identified as potential matches for those in step 5.*

It's a fairly hefty to-do list, but as long as we make progress on even a few of the items on the list, we should be fine.

After all, we have the rest of the year to make sure the matches we make are actual True Love ones.

Blech.

I still shudder every time I hear those words.

Or read them.

Or write them.

Or think them.

Basically, I'm shuddering all the time here at the FGA, but I suppose it could be worse.

I'm not sure how, but theoretically, it could be worse.

This is what keeps me up at night: knowing the day of the ball approaches ever closer, and that soon, I will have no choice but to face the True Love task head-on.

When that day finally arrives, I'm probably more nervous than the citizens of Midnight Falls who are hoping to snag a prince or a princess at the ball.

Finn greets me with a kiss in the common area of our wing and walks me to breakfast.

Max and Lia trail behind us.

Unlike me, they're thrilled this day has finally arrived.

Many of their matches will also be attending the ball so Lia is bubbling over with excitement at the potential Love Matches they might be making this evening.

"We could make history this evening," she exclaims. "The power of a True Love match can't be overstated."

And again, to that, I say blech.

The other three enjoy a hearty breakfast, but I'm entirely too nervous to do more than sip some water and drum my fingers on the table.

I am so far out of my comfort zone, I think I've entered the outer stratosphere.

When they're finally done eating, we head for the stables, mount our horses and retrace our route from three weeks before.

Once we arrive in Midnight Falls, the four of us make plans to meet up at the ball later that evening as we each have different tasks we must accomplish before then.

Max and Lia are both headed into town while Finn will be at the palace and I'll be at the manor with Cinderella and the Brighton women.

Finn is in charge of getting Lyle, who's made it clear he'd prefer to spend his time painting, to the ball.

My job is to get Cinderella there, even though from what we've observed over the mirror, Margaret has kept her promise not to spend a single penny on Cinderella, which leaves her with only rags to wear to the ball.

The problem is the rules of Faerie are very clear.

I can't give anything of Faerie to any of our targets and I'm also not allowed to spend any Fae coin anywhere but in Faerie itself. This means I cannot bring a dress to Cinderella nor can I buy one for her once I'm in Midnight Falls.

This leaves me with only one choice: magic.

Unfortunately, in order to create a dress for Cinderella, I have to interact with her, which means waiting until her stepmother and stepsisters leave for the ball.

It's not easy to observe Cinderella rushing around to help her sisters get ready for a ball she believes she won't be able to attend herself.

Finally, though, Margaret and her daughters are ready and leave the manor with the admonishment for Cinderella to clean up the mess they've made.

The minute they're gone, Cinderella crumbles.

She's been strong the entire time, not showing her sorrow or her pain, but now she sinks to the floor, buries her face in her hands and weeps.

I take a deep breath and pull my glamour back, so that it no longer shields me from sight.

I kneel at Cinderella's side and say, "Here now, it's all going to be all right. Dry your tears now."

Unfortunately, I fail to take into account the fact that Cinderella believes she's alone in the house and that she's never seen one of the Fae before.

Still, it's not like we look *that* different from humans.

Well, except for the ears.

And okay, our hair color can be unique.

Mine's pink.

Plus our eyes may seem a bit otherworldly.

But that's all really.

Okay, except for the mark.

I did forget about my dragon.

And the blade.

Still, I must say Cinderella completely overreacts.

By an awful lot.

She takes one look at me and lets out a shriek of terror, scrambling back as if I'm an assassin or something, which *fine*, I suppose I did spend the majority of my life training for that very purpose, but can't she see I've come in peace?

After all, I'm a Fae Godparent in training now.

Or something like that.

A Fae Godparent in training who doesn't believe in True Love and is quite aware she's just a tool for the throne, but whatever.

I'm still here to help her so I have no idea why she reacts so fiercely.

What happens next is really her own fault.

Everyone knows you shouldn't startle a dragon.

No matter how young they are.

But that's what she does.

To be clear, she startles me as well, but the real issue is the dragon, who chooses that exact moment to awaken.

In case you're wondering, it doesn't feel that great when a dragon peels away from your skin for the first time.

Actually, it might never feel great, but I imagine the first time is worse, simply because, well, you've never had that happen before.

In any case, it's a terribly itchy feeling and then it kind of progresses until it feels like a part of your face is literally just peeling off.

I guess the dragon is startled by all that shrieking, so she peels away pretty quickly.

One minute, she's dormant, the next, she's loose.

She's just a baby dragon, so it's not like she's even got that much fire, but Cinderella's shrieks get louder and she cowers in a corner as if a horde of full-grown dragons have attacked and are setting her house ablaze.

"Cinderella!" I cry. "Calm down. There's nothing to be afraid of. She's just a baby and I'm your Fae Godmother."

Yes, I actually said it out loud.

I claimed the title in front of witnesses (and by witnesses, I mean the target and the dragon), but what else can I do?

Cinderella will bring the entire kingdom into the house if she keeps shrieking like that.

"Did you hear me?" I shout, holding my arm in the air while trying to coax my dragon back down to me.

She's too busy flying around the room, investigating every single item in it, to pay me any attention though.

"I'm your Fae Godmother!"

The shrieks finally stop and Cinderella stares at me, mouth agape. "That's just a legend. There's no such thing."

I turn my head to the side. "Fae ears," I say, pointing at them.

"Surgery can do wonders these days."

Seriously?

"Blade mark of my clan." I run my finger down the dagger etched upon my cheek.

Cinderella shrugs. "Anyone can get a tattoo."

"Purple eyes."

"Contacts."

"Pink hair."

"Hair dye."

"Dragon flying around the room." I point up toward the chandelier where my dragon is currently attempting to light the candles there with her fire.

She's not having much luck.

I did mention she's a baby, didn't I?

"That *is* a new one," Cinderella admits. "I've never seen a dragon before."

I have to wonder if that means she's seen Fae ears before. "Dragons are very friendly. She was just startled by all the screaming. My name's Mari and I'm here to help you get ready for the ball."

Cinderella's eyes widen. "Oh, but I can't go. My stepmother said I have to stay here and clean."

"Are you seriously going to let that woman dictate whether you can attend the ball that the Royal Family has made clear *everyone* is invited to?"

Cinderella gets a mutinous on her face. "I'd be going right now if I could, no matter what she said, but I don't have anything to wear."

"And that, my dear, is why you need a Fae Godmother. I'm here to fix all that. So stand up, let me get a look at you."

Cinderella stands and I motion for her to spin around. She's wearing the same rags I saw her in the previous time I was here.

There is literally no magical power in all of Faerie that could transform those rags into beauty.

No matter though. I'm good at improvising.

"Right. You need to take a bath. Quickly though. While you're doing that, I'll work on your gown."

"Really?"

"Absolutely. Off you go."

Cinderella darts out of the room and I look around, taking in all the different fabrics available to me.

Tapestry on the wall.

Curtains on the windows.

Blanket over an armchair.

Tablecloth on the dining room table.

Yes. All of that will do nicely.

A quickly muttered spell extracts each from their spot without dislodging anything else along the way.

I line them up and begin the work of transforming four different pieces of fabric into one ballgown.

A bit of energy from the earth, a bit of space folded into the corner of one fabric and intertwined with another.

I pull and shape, sending some fabric away, thinning bits over here, and folding and buckling other pieces over there, sheering away entire sections, then pulling some back.

Basically, I make a disastrous mess.

No one in their right mind would wear this monstrosity.

I'm in desperate need of some help.

I am so not cut out for fashion design.

I grab my mirror and place an emergency call.

"Where are you, Mari?" Lia exclaims. "The ball's already begun. Finn's looking for you everywhere."

"We had to wait for the Brightons to leave and I'm not having any luck with Cinderella's gown. I need your help." I turn the mirror so Lia can see the horror show I've managed to create.

The noise she makes is somewhere between a gasp and a groan and every bit of it is horrified. "What is that?"

"Clearly it's my failure as a fashion designer. Please help, Lia."

"Give me five minutes."

Exactly three minutes later, Lia steps through a fold in space and lands in the dining room, swaying a bit from the abrupt nature of mirror walking.

"Right then. What fabrics were you using for this?"

"Curtains, tablecloth, blanket, tapestry."

"All of them? Together?"

"Well, yeah. I thought the more the better."

"Oh, dear."

Lia quickly takes over, nipping here, yanking there and before I know it, the curtains, the blanket and the tapestry are all gone and what's left isn't a ballgown, but it's not a tablecloth either.

She then does something with the fabric of the tablecloth, changes its composition or something, and it becomes almost sheer. She adds a deep midnight color and grabs a jar of buttons sitting on a side table.

She changes all the buttons into tiny, sparkling jewels and begins tossing them at the dress while whispering a weaving spell.

The jewels land and become part of the dress itself, adding a kind of glittery magic that immediately draws the eye.

"It's beautiful," Cinderella gasps from the door.

She's wrapped in a towel and is staring at the gown with wide eyes.

"Right. Let's get you into it. This is Lia, by the way. She's the fashion designer."

"Thank you, Lia," Cinderella breathes.

"No problem. I must get back." Lia turns to go.

"Wait!" I exclaim. "Shoes."

Lia chuckles and zaps a couple sneakers sitting by the front door.

They're instantly transformed into beautiful, glass slippers of a deep midnight color to match Cinderella's gown.

Lia steps out of the house and I'm sure zips away via her mirror.

I wish I could do the same for Cinderella, but unfortunately, she has to travel by human means.

She retreats around the corner with the gown and I spend the next few moments, coaxing my dragon back to me.

She's absolutely exquisite with scales the color of emeralds and bright purple eyes. I stroke her gently and cuddle her against my cheek until she winds herself back around the hilt of the dagger and falls asleep again.

"What do you think?" Cinderella asks from the doorway.

The gown is gorgeous and she's radiant in it. "You're absolutely stunning," I tell her.

"The dress fits perfectly," she says. "I love it." She steps into the glass slippers and proclaims them a perfect fit as well.

I notice while she was away getting dressed, she also did her own hair, which is excellent news since my hairdressing skills are about on par with my fashion design ones.

"Do you have a coach?"

She shakes her head. "My stepmother and stepsisters are using it."

"No matter. You can use mine." Anticipating this very problem, I had hired a coach and driver for the evening. "Let's go." I lead the way outside, help her climb into the coach and inform the driver, "Get her to the castle safely please."

I then turn back to Cinderella. "Listen closely. Your gown and slippers are made from Fae magic, but magic outside of Faerie has its limits. It cannot last beyond the striking of a new day. You must leave the ball no later than midnight or you will find yourself dressed in a tablecloth and sneakers. Try to avoid that, yes?"

Cinderella nods. "I will, I promise. Thank you so much, Fae Godmother."

I shake my head. "Mari."

"Mari."

"Now go have fun."

I step back and nod to the driver and they're off.

Chapter Twelve

I REACTIVATE MY glamour to conceal myself from human eyes, then mirror walk to the Palace.

Once inside, I scan the ballroom, searching for Finn.

The first thing I notice is that the princes, all three of them, are surrounded by both women and men. The only one who seems to be enjoying that state of affairs is the heir. Big surprise there.

The next thing I notice is how unhappy Lord Brighton appears.

He's watching Prince Victor with misery on his face and heartbreak in his eyes.

Right.

Time to start weaving a bit of True Love magic.

Just the thought makes me cringe, but there's no avoiding it. It's time to get to work.

I'm wearing my Criminal outfit of choice, which is a Fae skinsuit. It's easy to get on and has magic embedded deep within its threads. It's truly one of a Criminal's best tools in the field.

I swipe a hand down my torso and the skinsuit becomes a deep green ballgown. I then drop the glamour and saunter down the stairs, heading straight for the princes.

I slide through the crowd surrounding Prince Victor, hook my arm in his, inform his admirers that he's promised me this dance, then drag him off to the dance floor.

He doesn't protest at all, which tells me he's a target for anyone bold enough to walk up and steal him away. As soon as his admirers realize that, he'll never get a chance to pursue Lord Brighton (and by pursue, I mean stare at him longingly from across the room without actually doing anything).

This is where I come in.

"You looked a bit desperate," I say to him as I lead him around the dance floor, "so I thought I'd rescue you."

He doesn't say anything, just nods and blushes a little.

How adorable.

"I also couldn't help but notice how unhappy Lord Brighton appears."

His head immediately turns toward where Lord Brighton is standing, which tells me he's probably been observing the man as much as Lord Brighton has been observing him.

"So here's what we're going to do. I'm going to dance you over to Lord Brighton. From there, it's entirely up to you."

He glances back at me.

"You could just stand at his side and observe the party with him until the evening is done, *or* you can take a chance by reaching out your hand and asking your best friend to dance."

His eyes widen.

I then repeat something Finn once said to me. "Sometimes, Prince Victor, in order to experience True Love, you must first accept the possibility of it."

Impressed that I managed to say those words without gagging, I dance the two of us over to where Lord Brighton stands, watching us.

We stop in front of him and I reach up to whisper in Prince Victor's ear, "Take a chance," before walking away.

What happens next is entirely up to him.

I don't have to look back to know that Prince Victor takes my advice.

The explosion of whispers around me tell that tale, as does the look of utter joy on Princess Adriana's face as she watches her brother take a chance on love.

"Nicely done," Finn murmurs into my ear. "Dance with me?" Before I can even think to reply, he spins us out onto the dance floor.

We're still dancing when another explosion of whispers reverberates through the room.

Cinderella has arrived.

Finn and I watch as she descends the stairs into the ballroom.

A hush spreads as she walks through the many people gathered.

"Who is she?" Someone whispers behind us.

"I don't know. I've never seen her before."

"She's gorgeous."

"That dress is incredible."

Princess Adriana separates herself from the crowd and approaches Cinderella. "Ella?"

Cinderella smiles. "Adriana. I was hoping to see you here."

"It's been years, Ella. Since your father died. I waited for you to come back to school, but you never did. What happened?"

Ella steps closer and murmurs, "I was needed at home."

Adriana's brows lower. "The stepmonster refused to let you come back, didn't she?"

Ella shrugs. "She said it was too expensive."

"Walk with me, Ella. I've missed you so." Princess Adriana hooks her arm in Ella's and the two of them walk through the crowds and out of the ballroom into the darkened courtyards.

"Didn't see that one coming," Finn says.

"I didn't either, but this is wonderful," I say. "They already love each other."

"As friends."

"And friends make the best of lovers, or so I'm told." I peek up at him through my eyelashes. "I wouldn't know anything about that, of course, considering we were most definitely *not* friends."

Finn lets out a bark of laughter and slings his arm around my shoulders. "Come on. Dance some more with me."

He leads me onto the dance floor, pausing in a shadow along the way so that we can raise our glamour and shield ourselves once more from prying eyes.

As we dance, I search the ballroom for our other four matches.

Lyle looks miserable where he's standing by the wall, surrounded by females.

"Good job getting the youngest prince here," I say.

"Yeah, well, lot of good it's done us. He's turning down anyone who asks him to dance and he looks as if he might bolt at any minute."

This is true and quite the difference from Prince Adam, who

appears to be attempting to dance with every eligible woman in the room, and some of the men as well.

Lia and Max whirl onto the dance floor at that moment, weaving their way through the many couples dancing there.

I can tell the way no one is altering their dance paths as Max and Lia approach, that they too have their glamour in full effect.

When they reach our side, Lia says, "How's it going?"

"Not bad," I say, raising an eyebrow at the two of them. "How about you two?"

"Pretty good actually," Lia says. "A couple of our matches are dancing." She indicates a woman and a man as they whirl by. "We're struggling with Keri though. She's entirely too shy and is attempting to hide in the woodwork." She points to a figure in the shadow of a pillar. "Her mother insisted she attend, but then they lost each other in the crush of the crowd. I'm pretty sure Keri engineered that development."

I grin. "We have the same problem with Prince Lyle. Perhaps we should work together to get them to meet."

"Agreed," Max says. "You work on that while I take Lia on another spin of the ballroom."

Lia giggles as he whirls them away.

Okay, that's not cool.

Why didn't I think of that?

I glance at Finn, who grins. "I say we concentrate on matching their Keri with our Lyle and then we make them take Harriet and Bethany as payment for services rendered."

"Oooh, I like your style!"

Finn chuckles and we spend the next thirty minutes or so manipulating yet another match.

It only takes a small amount of magic—three spells to be exact—and a good dose of creativity.

We start with a spell to swivel a lantern so it casts light into the shadows of the pillar where Keri is hiding.

We do this at the exact moment when Lyle is glancing around the ballroom.

His eyes catch on Keri's figure and remain there.

We then cast another spell to dim the lantern's light, thus obscuring Keri once more, and prompting Lyle to move away from the people surrounding him in an attempt to gain a closer look.

Our third and final spell is the one that locks it all in place.

We snap the heel of Keri's shoe at just the right moment so that she stumbles just as Prince Lyle is getting close.

He leaps forward and catches her in his arms, then gallantly escorts her to a chair, where he kneels at her feet, snaps off the heel of her other shoe, then offers a hand and leads her onto the dance floor.

And so another match begins.

"You're a genius," Lia declares as she and Max dance by once more.

"Perhaps. We'll see if the match takes or not."

"If it does, you'll owe us one," Finn says. "Or two," he murmurs in my ear.

Lia giggles and calls out, "You got it," as Max swings her away again.

She has no idea what she's just agreed to.

"You know," Finn says, "that's five out of eight of our targets hooked up with a potential match. I'd say we're doing pretty well."

"Sure, but we've made zero progress with the nightmares."

We watch as Adam sweeps by with a woman on his arm, a look of pure arrogance on his face.

Two seconds later, Bethany and a gentleman who looks like he's sucked on a lemon dance by.

"I'm a very good catch, you know," we hear Bethany proclaim about herself.

Finn and I grimace at the same time.

"I think those last three matches can wait until *after* the holidays," I declare.

"Agreed," Finn says. "We'll just keep an eye on the current players and hope for the best."

He spins me around and dances me across the room so that we can take a peek out into the courtyard.

This is how the night passes—with Finn holding me in his arms, dancing the hours away.

I'm not admitting anything out loud, of course, but it's possible the evening may have been just a *little* romantic.

Especially as we circle the ballroom and catch glimpses throughout the night of Cinderella and Adriana talking in the courtyard, then of Victor and Steven dancing under the bright lights of the ballroom, then of Cinderella and Adriana dancing in the courtyard, then of both couples kissing.

"You know," Finn says, "for a Criminal, you're not half bad at this matchmaking gig." He sweeps me into a dip and kisses me breathless.

Long, dreamy moments later, he pulls me upright and grins at me.

My voice is husky and breathless as I respond, "Why thank you, kind sir, for both the compliment and the kiss."

He waggles his brows at me.

"I must say though, for a Godparent, *you're* not half bad at political machinations."

"Ah, don't say that." He kisses me again, this time with a gentle brush of the lips that has me craving more. "Really, I mean it." Another brush of those lips. "Don't say that. You'll ruin my reputation as a True Love believer."

"Don't worry," I murmur as I kiss him back. "Your secret is safe with me."

Thank you for reading

An Unlikely Match

Please consider leaving a review
on your favorite book site.

If you would like to be notified of A.J.'s new releases,
please sign up here:
www.ajculey.com/newsletter

OTHER BOOKS BY A.J.

can be found at www.ajculey.com

FOR TEENS AND ADULTS:

BENEATH THE WILLOW:
Sehmah's Truth
Jennara in Flux

SHIFTER HIGH:
Antler Trouble
Bunny Trouble
Prickly Trouble

FOR CHILDREN:

PICTURE BOOKS:
A Fairy's Job
If My Cat Could Fly
If My Dog Could Fly
Salsa Visits the Zoo
Taco Runs Away

TYRABBISAURUS REX:
Tyrabbisaurus Rex
Revenge of the Tiger
Zombie Bunnies
Tigernapped
Lockdown

ABOUT THE AUTHOR

A.J. Culey is a teacher, world traveler and writer. She lives with a number of very bossy cats and can be found at her website www.ajculey.com. She can also be followed on Facebook at www.facebook.com/ajculey.author and on social media @ajculey.

T-Rab from *Tyrabbisaurus Rex* is also on Twitter and Facebook @Tyrabbisaurus and can be found there when he manages to coax the laptop away from A.J.